a tour of evil

a tour of evil

Suzi Wizowaty

SLEUTH
PHILOMEL

Acknowledgments

Many thanks to Michael Green for helping make this the best
book possible, and to Ginger Knowlton for her faith and persistence.
Thanks to untold friends and family for their support of my work, and
especially to Gigi Wizowaty, Rick Archbold, and Nancy Garden.
Thanks to Natalie Babbitt, whom I've never met, for inspiration.
And most of all, and always, thanks to Joan Robinson.

PHILOMEL BOOKS
A division of Penguin Young Readers Group
Published by The Penguin Group
Penguin Group (USA) Inc., 375 Hudson Street, New York, NY 10014, U.S.A.
Penguin Group (Canada), 10 Alcorn Avenue, Toronto, Ontario, Canada M4V 3B2
(a division of Pearson Penguin Canada Inc.)
Penguin Books Ltd, 80 Strand, London WC2R 0RL, England.
Penguin Ireland, 25 St. Stephen's Green, Dublin 2, Ireland (a division of Penguin Books Ltd.)
Penguin Group (Australia), 250 Camberwell Road, Camberwell, Victoria 3124, Australia
(a division of Pearson Australia Group Pty Ltd).
Penguin Books India Pvt Ltd, 11 Community Centre, Panchsheel Park, New Delhi - 110 017, India.
Penguin Group (NZ), Cnr Airborne and Rosedale Roads, Albany, Auckland 1310, New Zealand
(a division of Pearson New Zealand Ltd).
Penguin Books (South Africa) (Pty) Ltd, 24 Sturdee Avenue, Rosebank, Johannesburg 2196, South Africa.
Penguin Books Ltd, Registered Offices: 80 Strand, London WC2R 0RL, England.

Library of Congress Cataloging-in-Publication Data
Wizowaty, Suzi. A tour of evil / Suzi Wizowaty.   p. cm.
Summary: The lives of an eleven-year-old runaway foster child, an old man with a tragic past,
and a worried foster mother intertwine as they rescue a group of kidnapped children
from an evil tour guide at a cathedral in northern France.
[1. Foundlings—Fiction. 2. Cathedrals—Fiction. 3. Kidnapping—Fiction. 4. Courage—Fiction.
5. Old age—Fiction. 6. Foster home care—Fiction. 7. France—Fiction.] I. Title.
PZ7.W7915To 2005   [Fic]—dc22   2004009540   ISBN 0-399-24251-1
1   3   5   7   9   10   8   6   4   2
First Impression

*For my mother, who loved cathedrals,
and my father, who avoided tour guides.*

a tour of evil

the beginning . . .

The first three days

In the early fall in northern France, there sometimes comes a handful of days that smell and taste of summer. Chilly nights yield to days so warm and light on the skin that parents forget that children have to get up early for school the next morning. Or perhaps they only pretend to forget, so they, too, can linger in front of their apartments or on street corners, watching their children run and tease and fight and roll on the still-warm sidewalk, laughing and wrestling. It is a slow, mysterious time. No one thinks about the storm that inevitably follows.

That was how this week began. Mothers and fathers finally called in their children, or followed them in reluctantly, sometime after nine o'clock, as slow, summery waves of dark eased the magic out of the day and left in its place ordinary night, fearsome, and a little too cold for comfort.

Few people noticed in Monday morning's newspaper the small box on an inside page that reported the first of the missing children. But on Tuesday morning, two more children were reported missing, and parents began to take note. They stopped each other on the street, or mentioned it casually but in a hushed voice while waiting in line at the butcher's. By Wednesday, though the days were still warm, and the sun seemed to mock their fears, more than a few frightened parents ordered their children straight home from school, and at least one anxious mother walked her embarrassed teenaged offspring to the school gate. Five children were now known to have disappeared—and five more missing children, who had been abiding with Madame Jouet, had not yet been reported.

Such is the way of the world that not everyone cares about things like missing children. Sometimes those who might care simply don't know. In a busy city like this one—no bigger than a large town, really, but a city by virtue of its unlikely possession of one of the great cathedrals of France—there is so much noise and commotion, so much hustle-bustle and hurly-burly, it's hard to keep track. Particularly of children, and particularly during those last heady days of summer-in-fall. Besides, some ask, is it not the way of children to run amok?

In any event, people have their own troubles. Alma, for example, and Barlach. Even Malocchio. Some unfortunate people seem to attract trouble; day after day it clings to them like a dozen invisible monkeys. Others take delight in causing grief. They work with a chilling determination that sucks the summer warmth right out of the air. What is left? Darkness. Wind. The sudden flight of frightened birds.

Only a great power can intervene.

day four

Thursday, 4 a.m.

Alma awoke and didn't know where she was. She always woke up with her heart racing, eyes wide open, as if someone had just screamed. She listened now, alert as a small egret. No one was crying. No one was even whimpering. There was only the deep, even breathing of children sleeping.

Slowly, her clenched hands released the sheets. It was her first night in her new foster home, a farm with lots of children, so many that one more or less didn't matter. What was it, her third one this year? Fourth? So what? She was the Great Adventurer, the Great Explorer. She was La Salle. She was Marco Polo.

She squirmed against the scratchy sheets, rough like country people, she thought. But the sheets were clean and they smelled nice, of tar soap and the wind. Maybe there was a hay barn here with a rope swing and places to hide, and they could all pretend to fly through the jungle, or across the tops of a forest, or swoop like swallows through an abandoned castle. Maybe she could teach the little ones how to talk to birds, or battle the pirate Jean Laffite—or maybe they already knew. Maybe it wouldn't be so bad here after all.

But wait. In her sleepiness she'd forgotten her vow to stop pretending. Remembering now, she sighed. Right. It only got her into trouble. *Face facts,* her social worker had said. *Stop making things up. You're not a queen, or an eagle. You're a foundling. A nobody. Get used to it.*

Alma didn't know how to go about facing facts. She wasn't a nobody, she was sure of that, but what was she?

Her foot bumped something at the bottom of her bed. Her new shoes! She'd forgotten them. The father had shoved them at her last night, saying she needed shoes for the city. She'd snorted and rolled her eyes. As if the city were dirtier than the country!

But after everyone was asleep, Alma had retrieved the shoes from under the bed. They were old, worn, tie-up shoes with fraying laces, but they were the first present anyone had given her in a long time. She'd slipped a hand inside one shoe, pressing her palm against the stiff, curled tongue, and rubbed the toe quietly against the sheet. She spit to wet the sheet. Back and forth she rubbed. Spit and rub, spit and rub. The toe, the curved sides, the cracked heel. She rubbed until her arms ached and she was sure the shoes must shine. In the daylight they wouldn't be dull brown and ugly but shiny and pretty, the envy of everyone. They were magic fur slippers, they were space shoes, they were Puss's seven-league boots for covering great distances—

Oh! She caught herself. They were just ordinary shoes. But she'd been dreaming of flying in her magic shoes, and she smiled at the memory.

Now, in what seemed like the middle of the night, she felt around for the shoes. She hugged them to her like a mama bird protecting her young, and dropped back asleep.

5 a.m.

Someone prodded Alma and she jerked awake. Her eyes flew open and she blinked against the harsh light.

"Come on, sleepyhead. *Vas-y.*" It was one of the older boys—she hadn't learned all their names yet. "Get dressed and hurry up."

"What time is it?" Alma stalled. No one answered, but the room was full of grumpy movement. She groped for her shoes under the covers. Finding them, she relaxed a bit, unfolded in her bed.

"It's morning," came a younger girl's friendly voice, muffled by a shirt stretching over her head.

"We're leaving in a few minutes and you better be there," said another child, not unkindly.

Where were they going?

"It's Thursday—Farmers' Market. No school," explained the first girl, as if Alma had thought aloud.

Could she refuse to go? What would happen if she

did? But Alma gave up the idea of resisting the trip. The Great Adventurer liked seeing new places, and besides— She stopped. She wasn't a great adventurer, she told herself sternly. She was just Alma the foster kid, going to Farmers' Market.

She sighed, and stuffed her bare feet into her new shoes. She felt a sudden raging tenderness: they were clunky old things, but she had rescued them from certain disaster. They probably would have been thrown out if she hadn't come along. Eyeing them more critically now, she saw they looked dingy in this cramped room with the bare lightbulb overhead. They needed the sun. Never mind. In the outside light they'd shine true.

After a hurried breakfast, Alma found herself wedged between two crates of vegetables in an open truck under the stars jumbling toward the Farmers' Market in the city. The sky had barely begun to lighten at one edge. The other children took up their places, bumping and pushing and finally curling around each other comfortably. A little boy climbed into an older girl's lap and snuggled into her arms. The girl rested her chin on his head. Alma had such a pang of longing she could hardly breathe. But she shrugged. She was only a visitor, after all. She wouldn't stay. Why should she care?

Were summer mornings colder in the country? Or was it that she had never been up this early? Wispy green carrot tops brushed against her cheek. She shivered in her thin cotton dress, but she didn't own a sweater, and no one had thought to give her one. *Why should they,* she thought. *I'm nothing to them.* She crossed her arms over her chest.

Her shoes stuck out from the ends of her legs like little boxes.

The truck bumped noisily over country roads. Alma watched with interest as, one by one, the other children fell asleep where they sprawled over each other like kittens, even those older than she. One's arm dangled over the cabbages; another's foot rested on the potatoes. It was hard to tell whether the children grew out of the vegetables or the vegetables grew out of the children.

The truck rocked along in the predawn light, through the broad valley of farms and vineyards, the blue Ardennes low in the distance. They passed now between dark, still woods full of silent winged creatures returning home after a night of hunting, and now between noisy fields full of frenzied, ecstatic chirping and chattering. Alma sighed. They probably all had homes.

6 a.m.

Barlach got up slowly before the light, washed and dressed slowly, and slipped a hunk of salami and a chunk of bread into a wrinkled, grease-stained paper bag for his lunch. His joints ached, especially in the damp. Only on the warmest summer days when the hot wind blew in from the south did his tiny attic rooms lose their chill. He inhabited them without seeing them, but he always felt the cold.

There were no mirrors in Barlach's rooms, and he didn't shave. Instead, every few months he took a pair of old, tired scissors and chopped roughly at his beard, leaning over a battered old trash can. He cut by feel, and the result was the same scraggly, scruffy beard as before, but shorter. He did the same thing with his hair.

His landlady came in once a month to sweep, and always scratched her head over the wood shavings piled in

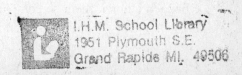

the corners and the stray tufts of wiry gray hair under the small dresser or the narrow bed.

Though Barlach was old—and not quite sure how old—he rode his bicycle to work every day. That is, every day but Sunday. On Sundays, Barlach walked in the city, collecting wood. He didn't go to church. On the contrary. Without thinking about it, he organized his endless Sunday walks to avoid every church in the city, including the cathedral.

On the days of the week, like today, Thursday, he rode to the center of town, where he swept the streets from seven in the morning until two in the afternoon. He was one of the last human street sweepers; most of them had been replaced by machines. Somehow, Barlach was still there, almost as if he had been forgotten.

Barlach never spoke to anyone. On Saturday afternoons, when the pay was given out, the boss sometimes tried to joke with him.

"Here you go, old man. Don't spend it all in one place." The other men, the ones who drove machines, laughed. Sometimes they joined in wishing Barlach a wild time. They were sure he had never had a wild time in his life.

Barlach ignored them so completely they wondered

if he'd gone deaf. He never smiled and each year he became more stooped, more forlorn. They used to ask him why he didn't buy a car, especially now that he was getting old—and the weather so terrible in winter! Barlach frowned but never answered. Now they teased him for old times' sake, and because they had nothing else to do. They lingered for a smoke, a bit of talk, a few empty jokes.

Today Barlach arrived at his workplace, walked his rattling bicycle through the alley around to the rear of the building, deposited his lunch and collected his worn-out broom from the owner, and set out for his streets. He patted the bulging pocket of his jacket once for comfort. His eyes flickered with what might have been mistaken for tenderness, if one didn't know better.

He had to find good homes for his children.

6 a.m.

By the time the first flicks of sun lit up the tumble of sleepy children amid the carefully packed crates, the truck had passed through the silent city streets and arrived at the market district. Here the sidewalks were broad and wide, and the warehouses had rolled up their storefront shutters to reveal more tables and booths inside. Almost in unison, the children woke up. Alma stretched awkwardly.

"Come on now, *venez*, let's go," called the oldest, jumping down. The others didn't speak much, either out of sleepiness or family habit. They emptied the back of the truck in silence but for an occasional grunt or "Watch yourself!" Quickly the booth they had staked out and the long table beside it filled up.

"Do you always come to the same place?" Alma asked one of the younger children.

"Always on Thursdays," he answered.

"Can I help?" she asked. No one answered. They all knew what to do without her; it was as if they'd forgotten she was there. Or as if she were invisible. She stood on the side in an agony of uselessness, kicking the curb furiously, but no one noticed.

End to end, booths lined the length of the street, along both sides. Alma knew what a Farmers' Market was like; every town had one—bigger places than this probably had them every day. Later the sidewalks would be so crowded you'd have to elbow your way through, making sure you didn't get crushed by enormous women with their string bags bulging with bread and vegetables. The older children would keep busy weighing produce and making change while the youngest kept the bins full and played in the truck. Alma had seen it all before in her exploring. At eleven, she had seen almost everything.

"Tomatoes over here. Green beans there. Claude, wake up. Turnips go underneath, there on the ground. How many times do I have to tell you?"

Other farmers and their families had arrived and were setting up their wares. There was more shouting, more trucks beeping, more slamming of doors and calling to neighbors, more banging of crates, more idling of motors, more giving orders.

"Over here!"

"Where's the change box?"

"Who forgot the paper bags?"

"Don't drop it! Easy!"

"Attention!"

At the first opportunity, Alma the Great Adventurer slipped between two trucks and disappeared.

7 a.m.

Madame Jouet's kitchen was painted bright yellow, with a blue and white checked floor. It was a large room as kitchens go, cluttered with boots and shoes of all sizes, stacks of newspapers, baskets of potatoes and onions. Dented copper pots and blackened cast-iron frying pans decorated the walls while bunches of drying herbs hung from the ceiling. It had no modern appliances—no dishwasher or microwave, no TV blaring from the corner. No matter how much the children complained, the fact was that she had no money for such things—or for computers or video games or cell phones. Besides, the children had plenty of exposure to these things at school. In truth, Madame Jouet preferred the sound of her own children laughing and arguing to the voices of strangers complaining from a box. She might be foolish, but she ran her shelter on a tight budget and what she cared about were raincoats and proper nutrition.

But this morning she was concerned about something else, and she didn't want the children—the ones who were left—to know just how very concerned she was. She wiped her eyes with pudgy fingers and frowned sternly at her reflection in the teakettle. For heaven's sake, it wasn't as if children had never run off before. They were children, after all; running off was one of the things they did.

But this time was different.

"Breakfast!" she called.

In the center of the room stood a long table upon which Madame Jouet set four ceramic bowls of hot cereal. Each one had a pat of butter and two lumps of sugar on top submerged in exactly half a cup of milk. Madame Jouet liked to count and measure; it calmed her nerves.

One, two, three, four, they stumbled in, still sleepy.

"Bonjour, bonjour," Madame cried in her great hearty voice. She wanted to hug them all, especially today, but Roc and Hannah believed themselves too old. The little one called Payah rested her bespectacled face against Madame's colorful skirts for a moment. She was a serious child with an unexpectedly big laugh. Gabi, the

redheaded youngest, threw himself upon Madame with his usual exuberance. She squeezed and kissed him until he pulled away. Hannah, taller than Roc and older by an important month, looked more worried than usual this morning. Roc, a passionate and impulsive boy, came in scowling, looking so much like an angry old man that it made Madame smile.

The children gathered at one end of the long wooden table and studiously avoided looking at the other end, which was noticeably empty. Madame Jouet held something behind her back. When she had their attention, she raised the bowl over her head with great ceremony and placed it like a holy offering in the center of the table.

"Sugar!" cried Gabi. Hannah and Roc rolled their eyes at each other.

"What's the occasion?" asked Hannah, as she whacked Gabi's hand, already inside the bowl digging for cubes. "It's not your name day *yet*." She handed the bowl to Payah, who waited politely. Hannah was a little *gendarme*, keeping everyone in order.

"Only because you're such excellent children—and the air is so warm and sweet today. Four lumps each."

But even this failed to spark any excitement in any-one except Gabi. They ate in silence, Gabi slurping loudly. Hannah elbowed him; he elbowed her back.

"*Tomorrow* is my name day!" Gabi reminded them shortly, bouncing in his seat. Roc and Hannah ex-changed troubled looks. Payah kept her eyes on her half-empty bowl. Madame Jouet pushed away from the table and began to sing.

"*Alouette, gentille alouette. Alouette—*"

"And everyone will come home then, won't they?" continued Gabi. "They always do! No one misses a name day party."

Madame Jouet swooped in to gather up the empty bowls, which scraped together noisily. She slid every-thing into the sink with a clatter. "Your saint's day? To-morrow's not really your saint's day, is it, Gabi? I thought it was next month. Are you sure? Finish your breakfast."

Gabi started to yell, not sure whether she was teas-ing him or not. "Saint Jean-Gabriel! The missionary! You told me!"

"Shh, shh," said Madame Jouet with a smile. She sat in one of the empty chairs and opened her arms. Gabi ran to her.

"In China!" he insisted, as if they didn't believe him. "The one who rescued abandoned children."

Madame smoothed Gabi's hair and clucked at him. "Yes, yes. It will be a perfect day." Gabi squirmed down and ran around the table twice and back to his place.

Roc and Hannah exchanged looks again.

"Perfect," echoed Payah softly. Roc nodded and punched Gabi lightly in the shoulder. The little boy relaxed and lifted his cereal bowl to his lips, slurping the last delicious sip of sugared milk. Hannah shook her head in disapproval, but Gabi only grinned all around.

9:30 a.m.

It was now a bright September day, warm with a hint of change in the air. Following her instincts, Alma had left the warehouse district on the outskirts of town, where the streets and sidewalks were wide and new and laid out in straight lines, and simply walked. Slowly the city grew more cramped and crowded around her. Here the narrow streets twisted and turned, angling in unexpected directions, and the gray stone buildings leaned their three stories over the sidewalks that were only wide enough for one person at a time. When two people approached each other, one of them had to step into the street to pass. Small cars and trucks rumbled over the cobblestones in bursts, slowing often and abruptly to avoid running over people, and honking a lot.

Now and then a tiny park with three or four small poplars and a bench squeezed itself into a triangular corner of a block, or sprouted in an intersection, and here and there a café spilled a couple of little round tables onto a larger expanse of sidewalk. When several streets joined and opened onto a small square, a dozen tiny tables and chairs crowded together outside a larger café.

Here in the old section, what bordered the sidewalks were not separate buildings but a continuous wall of attached structures—small shops like *pâtisseries* and *boulangeries* next to churches and stationery stores. In between, bronze lion's-head knockers decorated great wooden doors that opened onto courtyards of apartments.

Now Alma stood across the street from one such wall, listening. From here, she couldn't read the small print on the brass plaque by the gate, but she could tell it was a school from the shouts in the courtyard on the other side of the wall. A large courtyard, from the sound of it, with a couple of trees or at the very least window boxes. Through the black wrought-iron gate, only as wide as a narrow door, Alma caught glimpses of running, laughing children.

What kind of school was this, she wondered. She'd been to so many, the last one only a week ago. You never knew what they were like inside. The ugliest school she ever went to had a teacher with a voice like music who taught kids how to act out stories. You couldn't tell from the outsides of buildings—or people, either.

She stood watching, lost in a sudden wistfulness, until a boy and a girl, both about her age, saw her and approached the gate. They murmured to themselves. Were they about to speak to her? Should she yell to them? She felt unaccountably shy.

A man's voice announced the end of the recess.

"What are you doing out there?" the boy yelled. A car clattered between them. When it passed, the boy was no longer there. But she heard his voice. "Come on, Hannah!"

The girl, Hannah, hesitated with one hand still grasping a bar of the grate. "You watch out!" she called across the street. Then she disappeared.

Was it a threat? Or a warning? Alma watched the empty doorway until she heard an inner courtyard door slam shut behind the last noisy voices.

10 a.m.

Madame Jouet had been walking without direction for over an hour, peering around corners and into shop windows. *I don't know where to look!* she wailed to herself.

She was a large woman with a big head of curly hair, once red, now streaked with gray, which gave the impression of a hearty, lumbering creature of great strength and color, something between a giant peacock and an elephant. She wore a red wide-brimmed hat and several layers of multicolored skirts, winter and summer, which made her feel like an actor in the theater and not just a— whatever she was. A milliner. It sounded so prim, so lacking in dash, so *dull*.

Madame Jouet shook her head. She was not accustomed to worrying, or even thinking too much. It was not in her nature. She was glad for the hundredth time that she didn't have a television; the women in the *boulangerie* were always talking about the latest crises.

On those rare occasions when real disaster seemed to loom, like now, she counted. In the past hour she had counted nine bakeries, thirteen cafés, seven cake shops, five butchers, three paper stores that used to sell paper but now sold cellular phones and computer gadgets, two dress shops, and only one hat shop. No one wore real hats anymore, she mused. Thank goodness for the theater, or she'd have no one to buy the hats she made. As it was, she had to send them to a costume shop in Paris. And what hats they were, trimmed with plastic grapes and berries and bananas, and paper birds, with satin ribbons down the back or clouds of silk piled on top. Hats for dancers and actors—sultans, pirates, wealthy barons, and ladies of the night. From the sale of these hats, Madame Jouet augmented the meager subsidy she got from the city and was able to keep her children clothed and fed.

The cathedral bell tolled. Madame Jouet counted to ten. One more than the number of children she had currently under her care. Was *supposed* to have under her care. *Oh!* She bit her lip. Where *were* they?

She looked inside another stationery store. Nothing. She looked inside a dusty antique shop that had an old collection of windup circus toys she loved. Nothing. She walked around and around every path in each of three parks. Nothing.

Thirty-seven little stores, sixty-four old people walking alone, thirty-one mothers with small children, countless rushing working men and women, and not a single school-aged child out alone.

When she rested briefly on a bench, with her colorful skirts hiked up around her legs, she wondered whether she had the strength she used to. By most accounts she was still a young woman, but look at her! Maybe she wasn't capable of taking care of children anymore. She loved them so much, but . . . In the past two days she had come to feel rather like a very old and discouraged elephant. She fanned herself with her hat, which was her favorite, not only because it was red, but because it was covered in bright plastic cherries out of which peeked two small doves. It was the hat she wore when she needed courage.

When the cathedral bells chimed eleven, Madame Jouet headed for home. Her children would arrive from school at midday with burning appetites. They were like little birds chirping desperately for food—no, little birds at least stayed in one place. Her children were more like kittens, mewing plaintively—one note, over and over and over, *Mew, mew, mew*—but not in one place, no. They were in constant motion, tumbling and pawing and climbing all over one another.

But what would she feed them? Ah, here was another bakery. Maybe if she could bring home something un-usual, it would take their minds off it all. She didn't want them to worry. After all, didn't they have their own battles to fight? She knew children had secret battles of their own, which adults knew nothing about. She se-lected a loaf of bread in the shape of a fat bird, with a round chest and short, stubby tail. It made her smile; they would like it.

On her way out, still admiring her bread, Madame Jouet almost bumped into a tall, thin, scowling man. He stepped aside to avoid her, and gave her a scathing look. She gathered her long skirts with a flourish, smacked her red hat atop her curly hair, and swept out. She hoped *he* didn't have any children.

11:15 a.m.

The wet patches on Alma's forehead, chest, and shoulders didn't make her feel any different. She dabbed herself with water once more from what looked like a fancy stone birdbath just inside the main door of the cathedral, the way she had seen other people do. She had watched them from the shadows. But maybe she wasn't doing it quite the right way. No one in any of the families she had lived with had ever explained to her what you were supposed to do in a church or how it was supposed to make you feel. Now all she felt was foolish. And wet. *Oh well.* She shrugged. *Never mind.* She knew plenty of other things. Besides, here she was in this strange and mysterious place, right now—and none of *them* were!

When she'd first come in, she could hardly breathe. She had never been inside such a cavernous, magical place. You could put the tallest trees in the world inside it and they wouldn't touch the vaulted ceiling. Maybe it wasn't as high as the Eiffel Tower, but then it wasn't an airy metal structure, after all, it was built of stone— and way overhead, tall windows three times the height of a person lined the cathedral on both sides. And the colors! She craned her neck to see. A kaleidoscope of colors whirled around her in all directions. It was the most beautiful thing she'd ever seen. Red and blue and purple in different shades, and green, and bright golden yellow. The windows were lit up as if from within the glass itself, though she knew it was only the bright day-light outside shining through. The more she looked, the more she saw: the hundreds, no, thousands of tiny pieces of colored glass became figures, and scenes. Each window showed something different. And the stained glass windows cast glorious patches of blue and red and purple onto the smooth rectangular stones of the floor below, and the enormous stone pillars along the aisles, and the benches, and the opposite walls.

Someone coughed a long way away. Alma listened, and then she knew what else besides the eerie light made this place so different. Outside, trucks and cars roared through the streets, people talked and yelled, machines rumbled, car doors slammed, sirens and radios blared, everything clanked and clattered and roiled and jostled. Here inside, there was near silence.

Somewhere deep in the cathedral, a chair scraped over the stones. From somewhere else came the quiet echo of two low voices barely distinguishable as human sounds. Now someone rustled out of the bench where he'd had his private thoughts, and there was a soft, rhythmic clicking of shoes on the floor as he walked the long length of the nave toward the door. All the sounds echoed and faded away, as if swallowed up by the stone. It was both spooky and exhilarating. Alma didn't know what to make of it. Indeed she had goose bumps along her arms. She shivered. It made her think of— *No,* she told herself sternly. She shouldn't go imagining things. Nothing bad could happen here. The old stone walls made it safe as a fortress. She shook herself and set out to explore.

In one wall, slightly above her head, was a hollowed-out place with a glass front. Standing on tiptoe, she saw a small box had been set inside the wall. The box was edged with a curling, faded purple ribbon. In the center, all alone on a faded red velvet pillow, lay a small thorn, covered with dust. What was it? Maybe from the crown of Jesus, or from Sleeping Beauty's hedge? Alma shivered with delight.

Some of the stones on the floor were as big as a coffin. Some of these had names engraved on them as if someone were buried underneath. Alma sucked in her breath: she was walking on dead people.

What a wonderful place. She didn't need to imagine things; it was creepy enough on its own.

She stopped by a statue of the Virgin and Child next to an enormous column that it would have taken three people to reach around. The mother smiled sadly. The child, grave and pensive, looked off into the distance beyond his mother. Alma nodded at him with sympathy. He was so small. Did he already know that one way or another, through their own weakness or death or plain bad luck, mothers weren't much help? Poor thing.

It was a long walk to the altar area. On the stone floor, Alma's new-old shoes made scuffing noises that echoed in the vast space. She smiled at her shoes. In this light, they looked pretty. She ignored the rubbing at her heels. She wanted to like them. She wanted to like everything. She wanted to *love* everything. Or at least something.

A tall, thin man appeared out of nowhere and hurried toward the main entrance. He had a sharp face—neither handsome nor ugly but striking, if a little pale. He walked with a determined, pointed gait, as if he owned the place. As if he wanted to be bigger than he was. Curious, Alma followed.

"The tour to the crypt will begin in five minutes," he announced to no one in particular. But his voice was surprisingly loud and strangely commanding, and it carried, and shortly he was surrounded by a group of ten or twelve tourists, who only moments before had been so scattered throughout the cathedral as to be almost invisible.

"The cathedral you are about to experience is one of the finest, least known treasures of all Europe," he boomed. "From the original rose window in the west portal—offering some of the most splendid colors in the entire world—to the ancient Tomb of the Unfortunates, an underground crypt offering a gloomy glimpse of another time, the cathedral is a hymn to God and a lament for the devil. My name is Malocchio and I'll be your guide. If you'll please step this way."

11:30 a.m.

Barlach rested his stocky, twisted form on an old park bench. His feet barely touched the ground when he leaned back. He had collected his lunch from where he stored it—in the cramped closet otherwise known as his boss's office, at the back of a run-down old building. He extracted his bread and salami from the wrinkled paper bag. He took the salami in one hand and the bread in the other, but his hands rested on his knees. He looked like a statue, he was so still.

He thought back over the homes he'd found for his children this morning. He'd left one—the beaver with the accidentally sliced tail—astride a street sign by an empty parking space, so the next driver to arrive would find it. He left a bear, standing on its hind legs, on a windowsill, peering into a restaurant that wasn't yet open for the day's business. He left the bird perched on top of a bench, flapping its tiny wings (he imagined) at the traffic that went by.

The memory pleased Barlach and he nodded to himself. He never smiled. He remembered his salami and took a bite. He ate first from one hand, then the other. He was glad he had all his teeth.

Barlach lived in a quiet world. Unless addressed directly, which he rarely was, he could distinguish few sounds from the dull commotion around him. Conversations and traffic, barking dogs, clanking window shades, most sounds blended together into a soft rumbling noise, with a few exceptions, like the cathedral bell, for instance. No matter where he was, he could feel the cathedral bell hum inside his old body. But he could no longer hear the calls of birds.

The shade was nice here. He liked this park because it was clean. Oh, yes, once in a while there was a paper cup or a plastic bottle on the ground, but he picked them up before eating—and rarely was there broken glass or dozens of cigarette butts. A small black squirrel darted up to his bench and rushed away. Once again Barlach rested his hands on his knees.

This morning, when he'd bent down to pick up a

paper cup stuck in the grate around a tree in the sidewalk—the attention to detail that distinguished the human street sweepers from the machines—he left a tiny squirrel hooked over the edge of the short wire fence that was supposed to keep dogs away.

Now he watched the real squirrel. He considered throwing it a crumb, but the squirrel raced up a tree after a friend—or was it an enemy? So often it was hard to tell. The two squirrels chased each other through the branches, chattering away. Barlach finished his meal, licked his fingers, and wiped them carefully on his pants.

His tiny wooden figures would stay with their new owners as long as the owners liked. People might give them away, but the little figures would never leave on their own. This was one of the things Barlach liked.

With his penknife, Barlach popped open a small bottle of orange soda and held it on his knee without drinking it. The best part of the day was over. He had only one figure left. He always saved one until after lunch. Otherwise he would have placed them all within the first half hour. This way he put off the inevitable sadness. He felt it coming now.

He didn't understand it. He couldn't explain it, but

he felt as if something were missing. Had something fallen out of a hole in his heart?

Barlach drank his soda slowly. He folded up the greasy paper bag and slid it into his coat pocket. Everyone else was in short sleeves—it had felt like summer all week—but Barlach was prone to shivering. He hated to be cold. His fingers touched the remaining figure in his pocket. It was a dog, short and round, with a stubby bump for a tail. When he'd tried yesterday to carve a tail, it broke off.

A cloud passed over the sun. Barlach was suddenly anxious to get back to work. He dropped his empty soda bottle into a trash can and hurried back to retrieve his broom. Soon he'd find the perfect home for the dog.

12:10 p.m.

Alma followed as the tour began to snake around the cathedral. Malocchio was long and thin, with stubbly colorless hair and pale skin that made him look as though he belonged underground. At the same time, he looked like a man in charge. He had narrow, cool gray eyes, but when he spoke about the cathedral, his eyes lit up.

"There are many secrets in a magnificent structure like this, built on the remains of earlier ruins. The original building was probably built in the eighth century"—he walked slowly, now backward to face his audience, now forward, gesturing expansively with his thin arms—"and destroyed during the anti-church riots of the late twelfth."

Alma hung back. She could tell he'd given this speech a thousand times, and yet he wasn't bored. His face shone with joy. His long fingers curled and pointed with great flourishes. The way he moved, his tall, bony body looked to Alma like one of the long, thin souls writhing and twisting as they fell into hell, in the scene engraved over the cathedral's main doors.

At that moment Malocchio's eyes caught hers. Something flickered across his face and was gone. He smiled at her, as if inviting her to join.

Alma only shrugged. The tour continued down the side aisle without her. She could see he loved the place, and his deep voice pulled her in—but she wanted to explore on her own for now.

In the pews close to the altar, an old woman in black wearing a black kerchief rested her head on her arms. Near her a young man knelt hurriedly in the aisle before leaving, as Alma had seen several others do. A few other men and women sat quietly by themselves or together. One mumbled to himself—or perhaps he was praying. Two middle-aged women with cameras huddled over a guidebook. One of them exclaimed and pointed at a stained glass window high overhead.

"Everyone comes to see the windows," the guide said warmly. Alma whirled around, surprised to see the tour near her again. "The windows are indeed legendary. They tell stories richer than you can imagine, but no one knows how to read them anymore."

"I want to see the crypt!" a small voice whined.

The child's mother hushed him. He was one of only a few children on the tour. Alma had seen no other children anywhere in the cathedral. That made it a less friendly place, but still a worthy fortress. She stood apart, in the shadow of another great column.

"Of course *I* know the stories," Malocchio said, ignoring the interruption. "Look there. The man on the horse is Geoffrey the Third, who accompanied Richard the Lionhearted on crusade in 1192. But *Geoffrey*, Geoffrey of all people! Why did one of the bravest of all men choose such a shy little runt for a companion?"

"Excuse me. We *are* most eager to see the crypt."

Malocchio frowned, blinked a few times, and then smiled. He seemed to like the windows more than he liked the tourists.

"I'm sure you are. Allow me to show you the way and we'll be there shortly. You won't want to miss this one. Just look up now. In the lower panel there, you see the figure of the Virgin striking a man on the head with a hammer. You see her royal crown. She's unpredictable, she makes her own rules. And there, next to her—"

"How do you know all the stories?" asked a boy.

Malocchio eyed the boy with interest. "I have spent my life in the service of the cathedral. No one knows it like I do. You'll be lucky if you grow up to find so worthwhile a purpose." When not pointing, Malocchio held his hands together tightly, as if he could hardly contain them.

"Are we skipping the bell tower?" a woman asked politely.

Malocchio explained that one of the two towers was always closed to the public, and that right now the second one was closed for repairs. He waved vaguely toward the back of the cathedral, where they could see a barrier erected in front of the door. A blue-smocked workman emerged from the door, carrying a lunch box.

"Why?" came the same small voice.

Malocchio blinked. "For repairs," he repeated.

"But why?"

Alma smiled, in spite of her disappointment. She wanted to go up inside the tower and look out over the city. She'd seen the scaffolding around the tower this morning, and it had only made her imagine how much better she could feel the wind up there. She loved high places.

Malocchio evidently did not. Muttering under his breath, he led the tour briskly down the side aisle toward the altar.

The altar was protected on three sides by a twelve-foot-high iron screen—a Spanish influence—adorned with ornately sculpted flowers and birds. Behind the altar was the area Malocchio called the choir, flanked with wooden choir stalls, and behind that was a high stone wall. The tour followed Malocchio around behind the choir to a door almost hidden in the stone wall, but engraved with a scene. One of Malocchio's quick, restless hands paused lovingly on the flank of a wolf. Gently, with one finger, he traced the shape of the rabbit hanging from the wolf's mouth. For a moment, he seemed entranced. How fine it would be, thought Alma, to care about a place so much.

"Beneath the altar is a stone crypt. The crypt itself is not uncommon to this aged cathedral, but what it contains is indeed unusual." He hesitated, with his hand on the doorknob.

"The crypt is dark and damp. Some people find it frightening. I assure you there is nothing to fear, unless you are by nature a creature that fears small, dark places." He laughed a short laugh. "But anyone who would like to wait here may do so."

No one moved. The little boy who had spoken earlier twisted to look up uncertainly at his father, who smiled and nodded.

"Ah. Brave souls all. Very well." With his peculiar expression, half-sad, half-curious, Malocchio scanned the group. When he saw Alma, one of his gray eyes blinked. Was he winking at her? Alma didn't smile and neither did he. But her spine tingled strangely. She was not at all certain she wanted to see the crypt. Her heart beat an irregular rhythm. She'd never been underground and the thought of it made her palms sweat. Was she by nature a creature who feared small, dark places, like he'd said? What kind of creature was that?

But, she chided herself, what was there to be afraid of? Malocchio seemed kind enough, if a little odd. And wasn't she the Great Explorer? And after all, she *was* curious.

Malocchio pushed open the stone door, which, though hinged, moved heavily. Biting her lip, Alma watched him duck into the blackness.

12:30 p.m.

The group of tourists drew together. Alma, too, leaned into the group. The seconds ticked by. Maybe the cathedral had swallowed up Malocchio. But now a light blinked on in the stairwell—a bare bulb strung from a wire overhead, dim but enough to light the way—and a murmur of relief rippled through the small group. They laughed, shuffled their feet, and now, brave once more, they pressed eagerly toward the doorway.

The stairway was narrow and close, barely wide enough for one, with a low, arched stone ceiling—the tallest among them bent over so as not to hit their heads. No longer needing to hold on to each other for comfort, the tourists descended the steps in single file. It took a long time.

"Careful," murmured a mother. She yanked on her little girl's arm so hard, the child was almost lifted from the ground. Alma took a deep breath and squeezed in behind them.

Finally, what felt like several minutes later, they spilled out into the dark crypt itself. Alma wrapped her arms around herself. She wanted to fly up the stairwell into the light, but she hesitated. She'd never been in such a place as this. Her blood rebelled at the sense of walls pressing in on her, the heavy stone overhead. Slowly her eyes adjusted to the half-light and she made out the dimensions of the room, no bigger than five meters square. The arched ceiling was surprisingly high, held up by four columns. She relaxed a bit. Another wire looped along the edge of the vaulted ceiling and then up to the highest point, to hang still another single low-watt bulb. Alma who liked sun and wind and sky did not like it down here one bit.

The tour guide, who had not spoken since opening the door, now stepped out of the darkness like a shadow. He rubbed his hands together.

"The crypt is not a clean, well-lighted place, but it has its own joys." He smiled, but the shadows distorted his features into a grimace. "Look how it is built, of the heaviest, hardest stone within reach. Look at the ceiling's barrel-vault construction—Romanesque. The heavy columns. See how the ribs rise directly from the square capitals." He droned on, and Alma had a hard time listening. There was something soothing, lulling, almost hypnotic about the rhythms of his voice that calmed her. It was a beautiful voice, made for singing. Then suddenly he shifted his tone, as if the preparation were over and he were eager to get on with whatever came next and be done with it.

"But tourists don't want facts. You want poetry. Drama. Of course the drama is in the facts, but step this way. Careful now. Not too close."

They crowded around, squeezing Alma out so she couldn't see.

"Ooh, look!"

"*Attention!* Don't push!"

"*Ah mon Dieu.*"

"What is it?"

With an elbow poke to a man's stomach, Alma shoved her way to the front. There she found herself pressed against a waist-high guard fence, of the kind erected around construction sites. Inside the steel fence was a hole in the stone floor about a meter square. Four iron poles, anchored permanently into the stone at each end, crisscrossed the hole, creating a sort of grate, but one that a person might easily step through if he weren't careful.

Through the grate, she saw into another room below, even more dimly lit than the one she was in. Not even a room exactly but a space, a hole in the ground, the outlines of which were impossible to discern. It might have been only a few meters wide or it might have extended under the entire crypt. It was too dark to tell. It seemed like the kind of large, unremarkable cellar hole one might find in any large farmhouse. Except for its contents. Directly under the grate, lit by a small spotlight, was a great pile of bones.

No one made a sound.

Malocchio explained into the silence that the bones had always been there and no one knew anymore exactly to whom they belonged. He said this with relish, as if it gave him private pleasure. "They have acquired the right to stay by simply outliving everyone else who comes along." He laughed softly.

The right to stay. Alma sucked in her breath. She saw bones of all sizes—wide and flat, long and thin, unidentifiable short bones and bones that must have been shoulder blades. Tibias and fibulas, she remembered those from school, but were they arms or legs?

And ribs and hip bones and even a few skulls, piled on top of each other or strewn about in no apparent order. Here and there a solitary bone or a skull lay separate and alone on the floor, as if it had rolled off the pile and chosen firmer ground for its final resting place.

Malocchio was still speaking, quietly again in the same lulling voice, and Alma felt again as if her brain were filling up with cobwebs. The crypt was very still. She stared at the bones until her eyes smarted, but it was as if she were straining to see something that wasn't there. Her eyelids were heavy. She was so tired she wanted to lie down right there on the cold stone floor and sleep. She would have, were she not held upright by those pressing close to her.

The guide stopped speaking. The tourists began pushing toward the door, as eager now to leave as they had been to come down. Alma hesitated. She shook her head. But the cotton-candy-sticky, cobweb-thick feeling in her brain remained. She needed most of all to get above ground, where there was light and air and space to move—but something pulled at her and made her want to stay below in spite of herself. She didn't know why, and she couldn't quite make herself think. Feeling strangely stunned, she followed the others up the steps.

2:10 p.m.

On his bicycle, Barlach was not afraid to pass the cathedral. Since his path home took him through the old section of town, where the streets curved and wound and the pavement had worn down to the cobblestones, he sometimes paused to look at the great church. No one else in the city, besides tourists, stopped to gaze at a fixture that was as familiar as an ancient member of the family—like a great-great-grandmother, whom you revered but didn't have much to say to. Thus anyone noticing Barlach probably would have thought he was resting. After all, he was unfathomably old and stooped. Even his rickety bicycle, with its red paint faded to brown and peeling, looked as if it could use a rest.

When Barlach stopped, people gave him a wide berth. Perhaps it was because he looked wild and fierce, with his white eyebrows growing every which way. But Barlach didn't know what he looked like. If he had thought about it, which he didn't, he would have assumed people shied away from him for another reason, the reason he couldn't say. The reason so awful, if truth be told, that he could no longer remember it. He knew something had happened long ago. He had done something—or perhaps something had happened *to* him, he was no longer sure which. But he carried his buried secret around with him, unable to straighten under its weight. Now it was as much out of habit as fear that Barlach glared so savagely at anyone foolish enough to approach him. No stranger asked him for the time or a light. No one asked him for directions. No one asked him for anything.

Barlach was not a churchgoing man. He had not been inside a religious building on a Sunday that he could remember. But on this Thursday afternoon, when the September air was warm and the clouds had begun gathering overhead, Barlach found himself in front of the cathedral once again. He stared up at it without any more thoughts than he usually had, and he waited.

Some work was being done on one of the two bell towers overhead. Scaffolding surrounded it on three sides, and a small pile of stones and trash had collected at its base. Hunched over his bicycle, Barlach twisted painfully in order to glare up at it. He hadn't noticed it last week. What were they doing? Repairing? It looked fine to him, just like the other one, with its graceful pointed spire rising up from the square tower, its vaulted windows letting in the air and the birds. Perhaps they weren't repairing but cleaning. It was true the pink stone was tinged gray with soot. The sculpted curlicues decorating the spires were darker on the insides, and the gargoyles' features were obscured with dirt. He hadn't noticed before because it hurt him to look up. Barlach had little patience for the ways of other humans. But he was a careful man in his way; if they were cleaning, that was good.

Something fell from the tower into the rubble below. A stone, or a tool.

A tremor shook him. Disappointment, perhaps, or a vague sort of rage. But he didn't leave. Instead, he wheeled his bicycle past the construction fence and thrust it into a scratchy bush at the other side of the building. He patted the bicycle's worn seat as if it were a pet, and remembered the little, round dog he'd left on a child's bicycle seat earlier. Barlach had never had a pet, but he had a scowling fondness for his bicycle. It had served him well for so many years—so many years that he had forgotten why he took the vow that had bound him to it in the first place.

It took fourteen steps to reach the porch of the cathedral. Nine stairs, then a broader step that took two paces to cover, then three more stairs to the wide porch. The heavy bronze doors stood open, so it required only five more steps across the porch and over the raised doorjamb to enter the vestibule. Every step counted to Barlach, especially in the afternoon: he was tired. And he was not accustomed to climbing stairs, which required different muscles from those he used riding his bicycle or walking.

What was he doing here? It was inexplicable. But he plodded on. He entered the cathedral, scowling, and lingered in the shadows at the rear. He didn't cross himself when he came in; he had only the dimmest memory of someone showing him how to do it—his mother, perhaps, a long time ago. Now the stone bowl filled with holy water might as well have been a birdbath for all it meant to him.

In spite of himself, Barlach was drawn to the patches

of color resting on the stone floor, the soft, vibrant light from the windows overhead. He liked color. It filled up the empty place inside him. But the colors were as fickle as the sun, and inevitably they faded, and his temporary happiness slipped out through the hole in his heart, as if the chambers of his heart were too small to hold such fullness.

Ach. He would have spit had he not been inside.

Slowly Barlach made his way down the nave. In the rear of the cathedral there were no pews, only vast open space. After ten or twelve meters of empty space began the rows of chairs, and finally, after another fifteen or so meters, came two dozen rows of traditional wooden pews. Barlach passed up the rows of chairs and finally eased himself into a pew. He didn't necessarily want to sit so close to the altar, but the solid oak pews were more comfortable. Slowly, painfully, he slid down the pew, away from the center aisle toward the other end of the pew, which abutted a great, multicolumned pillar. A series of such pillars divided the central nave from the side aisles. Here he felt safe.

Again he waited. What for? He didn't know. What did he want here? What secret did the cathedral hold that drew him, almost against his will? What promise? Barlach was no more able to answer such questions than he was to ask them. He simply sat, watching patches of color brighten and fade, brighten and fade, as clouds outside blew across the sun.

2:25 p.m.

Above ground once more, Alma looked around at the pews, the immense columns, the vast space all about and the vaulted ceiling miles overhead—and wondered what she was doing here. She knew *where* she was, but why had she come here in the first place? And what time was it anyway?

She had a sudden vision of herself as the hands of an old-fashioned clock that had somehow got detached from the face where they belonged and were now walking around free but dazed. Unmoored. Lost.

Was it morning or afternoon? She couldn't tell. Maybe there was no time in here. Maybe she'd go outside to find out no time at all had passed since she came in.

But she didn't go outside. Instead she slipped into a pew, reluctant, even afraid, to leave. Dust motes danced in shafts of colored light. Alma watched thoughtfully.

A tremendous sigh from the other end of her pew made her start. It was followed by another, deeper sigh.

At the end of the pew, next to a clustered pillar ten feet across, sat an old man, with his unkempt white-haired face sunk almost to his chest. Now he lumbered to his feet, grunting and shuffling. He rubbed his thigh as if it pained him. He was hunched over and he moved out of the pillar's shadow toward the aisle before looking up.

When he saw Alma, he stopped short. His face collapsed. He swung around with surprising force as if to escape out the other side of the pew. But his way was blocked by the column. He whipped back toward her with a scowl so fierce, Alma caught her breath.

She stared back at him, defiant but curious, unwilling to move. She wasn't in his way, after all. What was he but an old man, rough as a mangy old dog, a *clochard*. He didn't scare her, she told herself. Very much. *I have as much right to be here as you do*, she thought.

The old man seemed frozen, as if lightning had struck and rooted him to the floor. Slowly now, never taking his eyes from hers, he approached, baring his teeth like a trapped animal, until he was a foot away.

Alma gripped the edge of the pew. He wouldn't hurt

her, at least not in plain daylight; churches were for everyone, weren't they?

Barlach's eyes bored into hers, and then, like a terrified creature with only one way out, he charged by her, with astonishing speed. No longer shuffling, the small hunched figure hurried toward the rear of the cathedral and darted out the door.

Suddenly Alma was hungry. Starving. *Like a baby bird,* her last foster mother used to say—the one who moved away. The thought brought her up short.

Her new family! She had completely forgotten about them!

Quickly now, as if the clock's hands had been returned to its face and were spinning wildly round and round to make up for the time they were unattached, she rushed for the door. She had to get back. They'd be wondering where she was. No matter what they thought of her—and she didn't suppose they thought very much—they'd surely be worried by now. And mad. She was suddenly certain she'd been gone ages.

With an unerring sense of direction, like a bird that knows the way south, Alma headed back to the Farmers' Market.

2:30 p.m.

Outside, Alma guessed it was midafternoon, though the sun had disappeared behind a surly gray cloud. Hungry and worried, she hurried through the streets, retracing her steps with barely a thought.

They weren't bad people, her new family. She had just slipped away to show them . . . she didn't even remember why, now. She'd been pretending she was the Great Explorer. And look what she'd found! Look what she could discover on her own.

But she was tired of being a foster kid. She wanted a real mother, a real family—or else she would take care of herself. (If only they would let her!) Besides, this latest family had enough kids already. Anyone could see that. They didn't need her. Or maybe it didn't matter if she was there or not. That was even worse.

She had spent her full eleven years living in different

towns and cities in northern France and even been to Paris twice on school trips, once to see *la Tour Eiffel* and *l'Arc de Triomphe* and once to go to *le musée du Louvre.* Paris. Now *there* was a real city. When she was her own boss, she would travel a lot. She would fly in airplanes. Maybe she would fly the plane herself. She would have dozens of friends to go exploring with and laugh with and talk to about the things she discovered, like the cathedral. And she would have a permanent home to come back to, a palace or a house by the sea, with her own bed and her own special things lined up in a row. Things like, like, a magic box you could reach in and get ice cream whenever you wanted, and scary books, and maps to secret places, and a ring that made you invisible. She would have clothes that hadn't been worn by other people already. Maybe even clothes made especially for her. And a warm coat. And maybe wings.

Alma crossed the last big street. She was getting closer.

Maybe she could tell someone in her new family about the cathedral. Only until she had a real friend, of course. Surely *one* of them would be interested. There must be one out of such a big group who cared about more than pigs and vegetables—mustn't there? Yes, and then she could show her new sister—or brother, it didn't matter—the crypt. Who wouldn't love the crypt?

The thought cheered her. She ran the last two blocks.

Smiling to herself, she rounded the last corner onto the street that a few hours ago had held the teeming, rowdy booths. She slowed her pace. She registered the quiet before she could believe what she saw.

The area was empty. The Farmers' Market was over. The empty plaza was a shambles of leftovers, a dirty wreck of bruised and spoiled vegetables and fruit littering the sidewalks and spilling into the street. There was no sign of her family. The only things left were things nobody wanted.

"What's the matter, *mademoiselle*? Lose something?" A young man, one of the few stragglers left, tossed the rest of his crates into his truck.

Alma swiped angrily at her tears with the back of her hand and turned away from him.

"Hey, don't worry," he called after her. "There's nothing here you can't get up the street at the store. Just cost you a little more is all."

How could they have left her?

Maybe they hadn't realized they'd left without her,

and when they did, they'd come back for her. She hesitated, glanced over her shoulder at the empty market. No. They wouldn't come back, she thought bitterly. They had no reason to. Why should they care about her? They probably thought she'd run away for good. She banged her fists against her sides in frustration. As if she had anywhere to go! How could they be so stupid?

She nearly tripped over a broken basket. Stupid shoes. How could she ever have thought they were pretty? They were hideous! They were the ugliest things she had ever seen in her whole life, the ugliest shoes in the world, and they pinched and rubbed terribly.

Dropping onto a step in a doorway, she ripped the laces open. With all her might she hurled the ugly things at a trash can already overflowing with refuse from the market. One beat-up shoe hit the edge and dropped to the sidewalk like a dead bird. The other lodged in the garbage piled on top, between a newspaper and a piece of broken crate.

Alma rocked back and forth. Her pale feet were wrinkled, with little indentations and creases where the shoes had dug into her skin. Her heels were red and blistering. How stupid she was to have worn them against her better judgment. But Alma didn't wail or scream or even pout. She only rocked and rocked and held on to herself for dear life.

Finally she stood, propelled by a hot anger. *It's better to go barefoot*, she raged, as she squished and stomped through the garbage on the sidewalk. Stomp, squish, stomp. She hopped as it tickled the bottoms of her feet. *You can run faster, and you can feel things with your feet.* Like this rotten tomato—splat!—squooshing through her toes. Or this cucumber that rolled under her foot, flattened, and—pop!—spewed pulp. Alma laughed in spite of herself.

Those other kids didn't know what they were missing. What a boring life they led; Alma could tell this from one evening spent with them. If they only knew what a remarkable person she was.

She had wanted to show them the cathedral. The crypt. Ha! She wiped her face again.

Trailing her toes along the sidewalk, kicking up flies here and there, carefully avoiding all disgusting substances like spit, Alma took stock. Here she was, on her own—what she'd always thought she wanted. No one to tell her what to do or where to go. No one to tell her to grow up and stop imagining things. She was eleven

years old, in a strange city where she didn't know anyone. But she was used to that. And she was strong. And
she liked being barefoot. And the sun was out again.
And, after all, she thought philosophically, she only really needed now the same thing she'd always needed—
a home.

But where should she even begin to look?

The way to find something was to look in the right
place. But first, she had the problem of food. She was
hungry. In fact, she was suddenly so ravenous she could
hardly stand up, let alone think. She swayed dramati-
cally from side to side, imagining herself about to faint.
She should have salvaged something from what was left
at the market. *No!* she argued with herself. She never
wanted to set foot there again. She might have to, but
not right away.

She passed an outdoor café. On a tray at an empty
table lay half a sandwich, apparently untouched. Without thinking, she snatched it and raced down the street.
A waiter with a white apron yelled after her and she
waved back, with her mouth full. He was only going to
throw it away, wasn't he? Or did he want it for himself?
But he could get more. She gulped it down quickly—

ham and cheese on a *baguette,* with mustard. Her favorite. Someone must have left it for her on purpose. Things were looking up.

Better able to concentrate now, Alma stopped abruptly. Would the police be searching for her? Should she go to them right now and say she got lost? By tonight she would be with the farmers again.

But what if they didn't want her anymore? What then? She'd be sent somewhere else where nobody wanted her. She couldn't bear it. No, this time she would take her chances on her own. She'd look for a home of *her* choice.

Enjoying her freedom now, enjoying the sunny day, enjoying the city, Alma walked. At first she only glanced at people, afraid of attracting notice, but soon she found they paid her no attention anyway. Now she searched every face, wondering about everyone she saw. Did this one have children? Was that one a good mother? This man looked too serious, that one was too old. Did this lady like desserts? She was nice and round. Did that one yell when she got mad? This one looked nice, but too rich; rich people never had room for extra children. What about this one in the big, crazy red hat and colorful skirts, who looked at her with such concern? Most of the grown-ups hadn't even seen her. She liked the look of this one, but, sadly, the woman rushed away, rustling her funny-looking skirts, though her backward glance seemed to say she would have liked to stay and talk.

Alma soon tired of this game. She couldn't simply follow someone home, after all, although she had thought at first about doing just that. *Hello, here I am, I've come to live with you. I'm skinny and impatient, but I'm good with little kids, and I don't eat very much.* No, no. *Guess what! You've won a prize! Me! I've come to live with you. I may look like a pain in the neck, but actually I'm really a princess in disguise.* No . . . *Actually I'll bring you good luck, because I'm really good, and—* No . . . *Well actually, I'm really, I'm fantastically—*

She flopped onto the next empty bench she came to. There was a tiny clattering sound as something fell from the bench. Alma crouched behind it to find the object. She cradled it in her hand. It was a tiny bird, no more than three centimeters high, carved out of unpainted wood. Its wings were slightly open, as if it were about to take off. Its head was smooth, its feathers gently ruffled as if by the wind. Alma pressed it to her cheek.

She slid onto the bench and leaned back against the wooden slats so her legs dangled.

How fine were its tiny feet. How delicate its tail. It reminded her of the cathedral—the carved birds on the altar screen and the wild animals on the sides of the granite tombs. But instead of iron or bronze it was made of wood; how easily it could be broken. She stroked its finely carved wings. She would protect it from danger.

Around Alma the city screeched and roared. The traffic, the shouts of drivers and of friends parting on the street, the jingling of bicycle bells, the clanking of machines, the beeping of trucks backing up in alleys, all the noise of the city floated over and around her in the soft September air like a warm wind.

And then came the bell. Into the afternoon spilled huge waves of sound, rolling through the streets and filling up space. Bonggggg, bonggggg, bonggggg.

Alma sat upright, astonished. The sound and its echoes surrounded her like a quiet morning mist. Like a magic breath. Like fingers of wind, it lifted her over the slate roofs and she flew, and she looked down on all the houses and all the families living inside them.

But the last peal of the bell died away, and there she was, on a city bench. It had only been the cathedral bell. The world hadn't stopped. People rushed back and forth in front of her on the sidewalk as if nothing had happened. But why hadn't they been frozen in their tracks, stunned by awe? Hadn't they even *noticed*? She must have heard it before, herself—but not like this.

It was astonishing. It was just her imagination. Or it was a miracle. Alma shivered and clutched the bird to her chest.

3:25 p.m.

Madame Jouet had lived in this town all her life, but she'd been a very little girl at the time of Barlach's accident. She didn't remember exactly what happened. She only remembered that if she ever saw him while she and her mother were walking along the narrow sidewalks, her mother pulled her close, murmuring something about *le pauvre*. Poor man. Then came the day *Le Pauvre* was riding by on his bicycle, and her mother grabbed her out of the way and accidentally swung her against the edge of a door that was just opening, and it cut her leg. She still had the scar. Her mother blamed the man and called him *Le Fou* ever afterward—Crazy Man—and Madame Jouet's childhood fear of him only increased.

Now that she was grown, Madame Jouet firmly forbade terror of that sort to enter her house, but its shadow stirred in her whenever she saw Barlach on the street. He was old now, but he looked wilder and fiercer than ever, and people still shied away from him. They must have had a reason.

It was because she was afraid that Madame Jouet now thought of *Le Fou;* she didn't know his name. She had looked everywhere and tried everything she could think of except going to the police, which she could never do. She hadn't given up—she would never give up—but fear needs a face. The face she gave it was Barlach's.

Everyone knew he hated children.

Didn't he snarl when they taunted him for his crazy hair and beard? Didn't he cringe and raise his arms as if to strike when they ran up to touch him on a dare? Didn't he avert his eyes from a woman pushing a stroller or a father carrying a sleeping infant the way the devil shied from the sign of the cross? Didn't he mutter furiously under his breath—saying God knows what awful things—when a child unknowingly crossed in front of his bicycle? This was what everyone said.

Madame Jouet wiped her brow with a clean, unironed handkerchief. Her broad-brimmed red hat kept the sun off her face, but the air had become sticky, and she sweated when she was unhappy. She had been walking and searching for hours, all afternoon and all morn-

ing, and her colorful skirts were drooping and her thick
legs were tired. She stopped at a corner, and counted the
people bustling about her. She stepped back out of the
way, leaned against a building. Seven, eight, nine.

"You all right, honey?" an old woman asked.
Madame Jouet nodded. The old woman continued on
her way, shaking her head.

And then she saw him. *Speak of the devil*, she
thought. It was *Le Fou* on his bicycle. Her stomach did
a little flip, and she lurched forward.

"*Pardon, pardon. 'Scusez moi.*" She pushed through
the crowd waiting to cross at the corner. "Excuse me."
She tried to follow him; it was as if she had conjured
him up out of her own fear.

She walked quickly. It was not hard to keep up with
him, he didn't ride very fast. She was glad she had never
been one to wear fashionable high-heeled shoes. She
had always been practical, sensible, counting and mea-
suring and weighing. Even now, rushing after a crazy
man, she wondered, sensibly, what she was going to do
when she caught up to him. Would she have the courage
to say anything?

She hurried past a girl who looked the same age as
Hannah and Roc, with a certain forlorn, rebellious look

Madame Jouet recognized—and admired. But why wasn't the child in school? The girl looked at Madame Jouet with searching eyes. But Madame Jouet didn't have time to do more than wonder. *Le Fou* had turned a corner ahead of her; she mustn't lose him.

But when Madame Jouet rounded the corner, there was no sign of man or bicycle. She walked the length of the street, peering into alleys and courtyards. Had he known she was following him? Had he tried to escape on purpose? Had he vanished into thin air like an incubus?

As relieved as she was disappointed, Madame Jouet only now began to shake.

5:15 p.m.

The cathedral was made of light stone with a pink tinge brought out by the early evening light. Flying buttresses extended from its sides like massive stone spider legs. The two graceful towers flanking the façade gave it extra majesty, even though the south tower was surrounded by iron scaffolding that made it look wounded. The entire façade was decorated with stone carvings—rows of stately kings or saints next to the arched central doorway, with its complicated and disturbing vision of heaven and hell above, hell full of tumbling, clawing, shrieking figures. And more dignitaries and more scenes around and above the other two smaller doors. It was a noisy, raucous world set in stone.

Alma observed it with new eyes. Could this be her new home?

Inside, she made her way down a side aisle. The stone floor was cold under her bare feet. Someone was playing the organ. The notes echoed mournfully around the space; even a blind person could tell how vast and empty it was.

Now that she looked more carefully, she saw things she hadn't noticed the first time. Tall, thin figures—more saints? or kings?—adorned the enormous stone pillars separating the side aisles from the center aisle. Who had they been in real life? Alma passed two women speaking in low voices and strained to hear what they were saying, but in this huge, cavernous space their voices were swallowed up.

Where in this enormous place could she hide? Not just in the shadows, which were everywhere, but out of sight. What about the bell tower? An escaped queen should live in a tower. She retraced her steps to the rear of the church. In each of the two bumped-in front corners was a door that must lead up to the bell towers. But on the north door hung a sign saying *Défense d'entrer*. No Admittance. She tried it anyway and found it locked.

The entrance to the south door was blocked off by three stainless steel stanchions attached to a thick red velvet cord, like she'd seen before in a museum waiting line. The doorway itself was open, and she could see stone steps spiraling upward. But just as she was about to slip under the barrier, a man in jeans and a hard hat appeared in the doorway. The tool belt around his waist held a hammer and several chisels of different sizes. He must be the master sculptor Malocchio had mentioned earlier, repairing the statuary. He closed the door behind him, locked it, and left by the front door without a glance at Alma.

Alma drooped visibly, like a soggy bird on whom the heavens have just dumped a rain. She sighed, and then shook herself. Where else?

She wandered down the side aisle, and then she remembered the small chapels that extended from the circular area behind the choir called the apse. She'd seen them this morning on the tour. Maybe there.

She crossed the fingers on both hands for good luck.

A movement caught her eye through the twelve-foot altar screen. On the other side of the cathedral was an engraved wooden staircase, winding up to a tall podium. In the base of the staircase was a door, unnoticeable until it opened.

Coming out of the door was the tour guide.

He paused with his hand still on the doorknob and looked around quickly, like a weasel peeking out of a hole, Alma thought. She ducked behind a chair. It had only a slatted back and he could see her if he wanted to, but he didn't seem to.

Alma's heart beat hard. She didn't want anyone to know what she was doing here—*especially* him. It was clear he considered the cathedral *his*. She doubted he'd want to share it with her. She'd have to be careful.

He sniffed the air, frowned, and strode toward the rear doors. He did look a little like a rodent, but there was an undeniable elegance in the way he moved his hands. His long fingers. And he knew so much. There was majesty in his knowledge. He was the King Rat from the Nutcracker story she'd heard in school. And she was the Nutcracker King with her own band of proper soldiers. She laughed to herself and darted toward the nearest pillar. She peeked around it: he was about to escape. She ran up the side aisle, past two more columns, and crouched behind a third—just as he glanced her way.

She held her breath. Had he seen her? Her chest heaved as if she'd been fighting a great battle. She wondered if he'd ever heard of the Nutcracker and what he would say if she tried to explain it. Maybe if he really knew her, he'd let her stay.

Malocchio took a step in her direction and stopped.

He held his hands tight before him. He considered for a moment, smiled a tiny smile, then turned softly and continued toward the rear of the church.

When Alma finally peered around the edge of the giant pillar, she saw Malocchio talking to a couple of tourists, with his back to her. She took a deep breath.

Ah. Now that it was no longer the two of them, the game was over. She sauntered back toward the altar.

She didn't see him gaze after her with a private nod to himself.

5:30 p.m.

Hannah finished winding up the ball of old string she'd been collecting as a present for Gabi and joined the others on the sidewalk in front of their house. It was an old, narrow stone building attached to similar structures on either side. Though used as a hotel long ago, only during Madame Jouet's lifetime had it acquired electricity and running water. But it was three stories high and the upper floors contained a lot of small, indestructible rooms. In other words, it was perfect for housing children no one else wanted, and Madame Jouet always called it "ours," and so all its children considered it theirs.

Gabi and Roc stood six feet apart with a long elastic band stretched around their ankles. Payah stood between them, the elastic wrapped around her legs, trying to jump out of it under Roc's steady direction. When he told her to jump, she jumped, but nothing happened. But Payah was nothing if not patient, and she kept trying.

"Will they come back for my name day?" Gabi asked Hannah, not for the first time that day. Hannah was the bossy one, the one with all the answers.

She had avoided the question until now. But Gabi looked so hopeful, the words popped out before she knew it. "Of course they will." She opened her arms wide, as if to embrace the warm evening air.

Roc shook his head at her in warning. She glared at him.

"You don't know how it is on the streets like I do," he said under his breath. Hannah stood next to him, watching the game.

"Let me have a turn, Payah," Gabi said. Payah dutifully took Gabi's place at the end, inside the elastic band, and Gabi moved into the center. He deftly went through several maneuvers until he, too, got stuck.

"They're just off playing hooky," Hannah said. She spoke quietly. "Having an adventure."

"All five of them?" Roc said. "Jump, Gabi. Try again."

Hannah relieved Payah of her job holding the elastic.

Payah sat on the steps of their building, watching and listening.

"It's so—so irresponsible!" burst out Hannah. She didn't know what made her madder—Roc acting like something terrible had happened, or the missing children not showing up for two days.

"What is?" asked Gabi, stopping mid-game.

"Nothing," said Roc. "Why'd you stop? You almost made it all the way through. Keep going."

"You used to run away all the time, too," Hannah said under her breath to Roc. "Before." She would have liked to blame him. Or anybody.

"Yeah." Roc shrugged. "But this is different."

"No one would miss Gabi's name day on purpose," Payah agreed, from the stoop.

Hearing his name, Gabi smiled at her. He gathered his strength, jumped, lifted both feet ten centimeters off the ground, and with a wild twist freed himself of the elastic. The other three clapped. Gabi shouted in triumph.

Just then Madame Jouet called the children in for dinner.

Gabi jumped outside the elastic, and he and Payah raced inside. Roc wound up the long gray strip, frayed at the edges. "We better start looking for them," he said to Hannah.

"Just a few months ago, two of them ran off for three days."

"I know, Hannah, and the police threatened to shut the house down. They said she couldn't handle kids. Don't you remember?"

"Of course. But they wouldn't do that." Hannah tried to sound confident, but her voice was full of doubt. She so wanted things to be all right.

"Maybe they would and maybe they wouldn't. But something is wrong. Something is different. I can feel it." He kicked at the doorstep, waiting for her to agree. "I want to start looking tonight."

"Tonight! We can't. They might come home while we're gone. Let's give them one more night. Tomorrow. Tomorrow I'll go with you. We'll all go."

5:45 p.m.

Sticking out from the apse behind the choir was a series of small chapels big enough, from what Alma could see, for two or three people to pray in without bumping elbows. Except that it seemed that you weren't actually supposed to go into any of them: each one was blocked off by a low barrier, a sort of fence made out of iron or wood. It seemed you were supposed to pray in *front* of them, not *in* them. In front of each fence was a long, low bench for kneeling.

Alma looked about her casually, as if she were simply interested in her surroundings. But there were few worshippers or tourists in the cathedral at this hour, and no one seemed to notice her. She fingered the little bird in the pocket of her dress for good luck.

The first little chapel had a wooden gate in its fence, with a wide rim on which sat a flat iron stand full of several dozen squat candles. Dozens of tiny flames flickered

in the dim light. Inside was an altar, and on the sur-
rounding walls were painted scenes. Frescoes, the tour
guide had called them. Jesus with a crowd of harried
beggars pulling at him. Jesus on the cross being poked
in the side with a long pole, the blood starting to ooze
out. Jesus being taken down from the cross for a group
of wailing women in black.

The paintings made Alma's palms sweat and she had
to let go of the bird to wipe them off.

The next chapel was better. Its walls were lined with
sculptures of grave, still saints who might look after her,
she thought. The altar was stone, too. But no, it wasn't
an altar. On top of it lay a stone knight with his arms
folded across his chest. Maybe a king. It must be a
sarcophagus--that's what the tour guide had called a
similar thing elsewhere. Alma didn't want to be living
with any dead people. She moved on.

The next one held another sarcophagus. But here
only a few candles burned on the tray in front. Poor
man. Maybe she would light one for him, too. But she
hesitated. Was the candle supposed to be for the dead
person in the chapel or for someone religious like Jesus
or Mary? Or was it supposed to be for someone you
knew? There was a small wooden donation box next to

the stack of unlit candles. *Well, if you have to pay for them* . . . Alma didn't have any money.

The fourth chapel, the one in the middle—there were seven in all—was the only one without a tray full of candles in front. Instead, just inside the wrought-iron railing a six-foot-tall bronze candelabra stood guard like a sentry. Its seven tapers were unlit.

Alma liked this. She thought fewer people would stop to pray here since they couldn't light their own candles. But there was a man kneeling on the stool now. His head was bent over his arms and his forehead touched the railing. Alma waited in the shadows for him to leave.

On the other side of the railing was the simplest altar of all. There were three painted wooden panels on the back wall, with gold borders. One showed Adam and Eve, with no sign of the snake. Alma didn't recognize what the other two were about. She liked Adam and Eve all right. And because the other walls were plain, you could see the light from the stained glass windows high above reflected on the stone. She loved the colored light.

The altar itself appeared to be a simple table covered with a heavy white cloth that fell all the way to the ground. Under it lay a faded rug with worn fringe.

Alma hummed impatiently, eager to investigate, then

cocked her head. Something was different. Where was the organ music? She hadn't noticed when it stopped. Sounds were tricky in here; they sneaked up on you when you didn't expect them.

The kneeling man rose stiffly and moved on, but a young couple strolled by, gazing at each other more than at the chapels. Alma hadn't heard them coming. She studied the paintings, waiting. Finally the pair rounded the bend and disappeared. It was another advantage of this spot. Since it was directly behind the choir, it was more protected than the others. She could slip in and out more easily, without anyone seeing her.

With a quick glance over both shoulders, she hopped over the low railing, leaped the two steps to the altar, and ducked behind it. No one must hear her, either. She waited, but it was hard to tell where sounds came from in here, or where they went. She heard nothing nearby. Barefoot, Alma herself made little sound. Now she took her time. Gently, almost reverently, she lifted the altar cloth. It was a smooth, light material she had never felt before—not heavy as she had thought—silk, maybe, and it had gold tassels in the corners. She crawled underneath it.

If it was dim in the cathedral, it was even dimmer in

here, under the table. The small amount of evening light filtered eerily through the cloth. The heavy wooden table over her head was perhaps a meter wide and a meter and a half long. She could sit up comfortably, without bumping her head, and stretch out without being seen. The table itself stood on a large, oval maroon rug. It was like a tiny robbers' cave, or a mysterious ancient tent, something out of *The Arabian Nights*, which one of her foster mothers used to read to her. Alma was the head robber, a sultan, queen of the night.

Aside from the fact that she had no fellow robbers, or guests, or knights to rule over or fight, or even play with, it was the perfect home.

Alma wanted to do something special to make the cave hers. Moving carefully so as not to disturb the cloth hanging around her, she spit into a corner of the rug, just inside the table leg. She started to make an *X*, then drew an *A* instead. *A* for Alma. She repeated the procedure in the other three corners.

Something was missing. It needed something to . . . to watch over it. Some kind of talisman for inside, the way the candelabra guarded the chapel as a whole. But she didn't have anything. *No, wait.* The little bird in her pocket. She brought it close to her face and examined it again. It was so small, but it looked real, the way the wind rippled its feathers, the way it leaned forward into the wind. It was more than real. It was a moment of forever. For the first time, she wondered who could have made it.

The bird wouldn't stand on the rug, so Alma set it on its tail feathers, feet protruding in front of it, undignified, like a duck landing on a lake. She started to laugh out loud and caught herself just in time. She had best be quiet as a little wooden bird herself. In her mind she consoled the hapless, abandoned creature. *No one could love you more than I do.*

Satisfied, she sat back on her heels, humming again—and again caught herself. Never mind, she could sing outside. She felt like singing *loud.*

9:30 p.m.

There might have been more of a public outcry about the five children known to be missing, rather than only private worry, had it not been discovered that two of the children were Roma—Gypsies—and the other three were Moroccan, Tunisian, and Algerian. *La Belle France,* like many countries, has had its share of small-minded leaders, and it happened that a vocal national politician at the time blamed immigrants for many things wrong with France. It might as well have been *les Juifs* or *les Nègres*—and often it was. In any event, for whatever the reason—laziness, political convenience, or sheer stupidity—local public officials remained unmoved. One was quoted as saying, "The poor will always be with us," and another suggested that immigrant children might be safer back where they came from. The desperate cries of small communities went unheard.

Alma knew none of this. She might not have realized

the significance of the events even if she had. In her world of foster homes and state care, children ran away all the time. What she did know was that she had to watch out for the police if she didn't want to be taken back. She didn't want to be taken *back* anywhere. Not back to the farm she'd never come to know, not back to any of the other foster families she'd lived with during her eleven years, and not back to one of those Juvenile Homes they put you in when no one else will take you. She'd only been in one once, a long time ago, but it was so cold at night, under the thinnest little blanket imaginable, she couldn't even sleep. Not fit for an old *clochard*, let alone a Great Explorer or a Warrior Queen.

No, not back. Forward into new adventures! She wasn't just a pair of old shoes to be passed around from person to person. She was a pair of ruby slippers! Seven-league boots! She wanted to live with people who wanted her or with nobody at all.

Avoiding the police in this town was not as difficult as it might have been. Alma didn't know it but the force consisted of only six men. One oversaw the office, and one slept in the basement guarding prisoners brought in the night before for drunkenness or creating a nuisance. The other four alternated watching over the townspeople night and day, two at a time. Of course it would have taken only one *gendarme* to catch her.

That Thursday evening the streets were not crowded, in spite of the soft warmth still in the air. The earlier breeze had died down. Streetlamps blinked on one by one. Only once did Alma see a policeman, and she easily changed her course. She was beginning to know the streets in the old section well.

By nine-thirty she had managed to scrounge for herself an adequate dinner: two bruised but otherwise perfectly good apples and a carrot from the ground next to a corner grocery—they must have fallen off the bins standing outside—and four rolls swiped from outdoor cafés. She wasn't stealing, she told herself, she was taking leftovers. She had no moral objection to stealing what she needed, but she knew she would attract less attention if she took food that had rolled onto the sidewalk or had been paid for but left on a plate. She had no qualms about eating someone else's leftovers, either. Food was food, and she was free now and having an adventure.

Alma arrived back at the cathedral in the dark. The streetlight in front of the cathedral was out. A special spotlight had been set up alongside the construction fence, but it only shined onto half of the façade. The other half was shadowed, giving the cathedral the odd look of a two-toned mask, half black, half white.

Alma lingered across the street, admiring her new home with delight. She wished she had someone to tell: *Isn't it beautiful? It's where I live!* She shivered in spite of herself. It *was* a little scary, she had to admit, looming so huge in the dark, but didn't that make it all the more magnificent? And weren't churches sanctuaries? Didn't they keep out bad people and give refuge to good?

Suddenly she was terribly tired and wanted only to find her chapel and sleep. She climbed the steps, counting them one by one as, unknown to her, Barlach had earlier. Over the main door, the monsters falling into hell with their howling faces and ugly grimaces, now half in shadow, were more real than ever. She tugged on the iron handle.

Strangely, the door wouldn't open. Could it be locked? She tried the other door, on the right. She should have got here earlier! She tried the door on the left. Why were the doors locked? She pulled with all her might, pushed and pulled again. It didn't budge. Was it stuck? She tried the first two doors again, and then again the third.

Cathedrals were supposed to stay open all the time!

Overhead the shrieking souls tumbling over each other seemed to leer at her. Alma leaned her forehead against the cold bronze. She had to think. There must be other doors.

She descended the long steps, not counting now, and walked around the block, which the cathedral occupied entirely. Indeed, the north transept had a door. But she discovered it was locked. She continued her trek around the building. The door in the south transept was locked, too.

"There's no use rattling the door, *ma petite,*" a woman called to her from the sidewalk. "There'll be no one in there at this hour. Best go on home."

Reluctantly, Alma released the handle. She felt the woman's eyes on her as she trudged away, as if she were going home after all. When she glanced over her shoulder, the woman had disappeared. Alma returned numbly to the front of the cathedral.

She sat by the left door in the shadows, with her knees drawn in tight to her chest. Her hands and feet were cold, though the night still had in it a few hours' warmth. This was her home, the only one she had left, the one home she really wanted, and she couldn't get into it. It was maddening. She wiped away tears of rage.

Stop that, she told herself furiously. But it had been a long day and she was tired. And she didn't know what to do. She didn't feel like a great explorer anymore. Or a queen.

The streets were quiet but for an occasional truck rumbling by. A *gendarme* approached on the sidewalk below. He glanced in Alma's direction, but he didn't seem to see her. Perhaps it was too dark, or perhaps she was too little to care about. Just a kid. Alma curled into a ball, as small as she could get, before the door. She wished she had her little bird, but it was guarding her new home under the altar table. She pressed her fists to her mouth. She hoped it would be fine all by itself, with no one to take care of it. She hoped it wouldn't be too lonely, or too scared.

10 p.m.

Barlach sat on the edge of his bed, penknife in one hand, half-finished figure in the other. The old, beat-up tin trash can between his knees had caught most, but not all, of the tiny wood shavings. The rest lay scattered at his feet. Later he would scoop them up with his hand, because his landlady didn't like them. He knew she thought he was odd, but he didn't care. He had always been alone.

Barlach knew he should be asleep by now. He kept to a regular schedule, without much to nudge him off track. But tonight he heard a knocking in his mind, as if something wanted to come in. Something, some thought, wanted attention and he didn't know what it was. He waited. It was the second strange thing that had happened today.

The first was his run-in with the little girl in the cathedral. It had scared him so badly it made the pain come in his heart. Afterward, he'd pedaled home as he always did, avoiding cars and pedestrians automatically, giving both a wide berth. He didn't know why he'd been so frightened. Everything else had been the same; it was a temperamental afternoon, strangely warm for September, but otherwise unremarkable. He didn't like to think about it.

And now it was night. Barlach had eaten his simple meal and rested. He took up his knife and a suitable piece of wood he'd found earlier in the day, in a small park near where he was sweeping. Gently he stripped the bark from the branch. It was always easier to strip wood in the fall. As he worked, he waited patiently for whatever needed his attention to reveal itself.

A picture floated into his head.

This was different from seeing an animal trapped inside a piece of wood—a tiny squirrel, or a bird with uplifted wings—and carving away the wood to find it. This was a picture floating like a silken handkerchief from the sky. It settled in his brain like on a clothesline and hung there. It was a picture of the girl in the cathedral. He saw her sitting in the pew, her feet drawn up in front of her. He saw her thin white dress and boxy brown shoes. He saw her wide eyes. She'd been angry, or frightened. But why? Barlach was confused.

Barlach was not accustomed to turning things over and over in his mind. Too much thinking hurt him. But this picture wouldn't leave. He had to do something. He was tired, but he must act. Reluctantly, driven by something he didn't understand, Barlach left his safe, gloomy rooms.

A few minutes later, he found himself on his wobbly bicycle, riding down familiarly bumpy, uneven streets in the dark. Buildings were shuttered for the night. Light spilled occasionally from second- or third-story windows and flickered from TV screens he couldn't hear, but the streets were empty. He rode in and out of pools of light from his own cheap neighborhood to the center of town, the old section.

He didn't know what he was going to do, but he knew where he was going. There was something he had to take care of. But what was it?

When he arrived at the cathedral, Barlach stood astride his bicycle, panting slightly, scowling at its strange half-dark, half-lighted façade. He could have lain in the gutter and slept right now, he was so weary. But he was no bum. He leaned his bicycle against the nearest lamppost in the dark—with the burned-out light—and slowly climbed the steps.

In his tired state the climb was torturous. He tripped after only a few steps. He caught himself with his hands, and scraped his palms on the stone, but they were callused from years of handling a broom. On the outside he was tough. It was his joints, his insides, that hurt. He righted himself with a quiet groan and kept climbing, eyeing his feet suspiciously as if they might betray him at any moment.

At the top of the stairs, he closed his eyes to better catch his breath. Again he saw the picture in his head, gently waving, not like a photograph, but like a painting on silk. Soft. He watched it for a moment, and when he opened his eyes, he was surprised at where he was. And at what he saw.

It was the little girl.

In the dark in front of the door, she was nothing but a crumpled, curled-up little animal, with her hands tucked under her head. A small human version of a sleeping dog or a cat he might carve from a chunk of wood. Her arms were bare and she had no shoes. Asleep she didn't terrify him, but still he trembled.

Quietly, without thinking, Barlach pulled off his old jacket. He hesitated. How shabby and worn it was; why hadn't he noticed this until now? But it was warm. Ever so gently, as if covering a wounded bird, and holding his breath so as to make no sound, he draped the old jacket lightly over her.

11 p.m.

It had taken Malocchio longer than usual to get home to his shabby book-lined rooms in the evening. He'd had extra things to take care of at the cathedral to prepare for tomorrow, his last day, the day of reckoning. But now he was home, and, excited as he was, he mustn't neglect his studying.

But the squirrel!

Malocchio had devoted his life to studying the history and art and architecture of the cathedral. He knew as much about the political intrigue that had taken place around its construction hundreds of years ago as he did about the snake paintings in its chapels—paintings other people thought were about Adam and Eve. But he knew better. He knew, too, the story of every sculpted saint, and every devil. The devil as goat, the devil as whale. The monstrous stone gargoyles keeping watch from atop the cathedral . . . what were they if not devils? Devilish friends, friends to devils. When Malocchio was not leading tours, he scoured used bookshops for more information. The darker and dustier the shop, the more likely he was to find the kind of information he liked best. He'd never known why he was so drawn to these darker tales. Perhaps, he thought now, he'd sold his soul to the devil without realizing it. Never mind. It was too late now.

Malocchio loved his books, but after he'd read one, he didn't have much use for it. He didn't want anyone else to have it, so he couldn't give it away. But all the care he could muster for old things was reserved for the cathedral, and his bookcases were as dusty and cobwebbed as the contents of an old tomb. Malocchio didn't mind keeping company with spiders. He felt sympathy for maligned creatures. He liked folktales about evil sisters who spewed lizards and toads and bats from their mouths.

What Malocchio disliked almost as much as he disliked flowers, and sunlight and high places, was finding little wooden animals around the city. It had happened regularly over the years. Sometimes he found two or three a month—a tiny dog, or a bear rearing up on its hind legs, or a deer in flight. It enraged him. He couldn't explain his rage, he only knew that everything about these creatures was wrong. They were too delicate, for one thing. And besides, they weren't really art, they were just idiotic little creatures. In any case, they had no right to live. The only beautiful things that had a right to exist were in the cathedral. Only in the cathedral. Finding the tiny sculptures distressed Malocchio so much, sometimes he couldn't even read.

Tonight was one of those nights. With an angry cry, he threw his book across the room. He took from his pocket the squirrel he'd found today and placed it on the floor. From atop the tall, dusty bookcase he retrieved a small hammer. He built a sort of low wall out of mildewed books to surround the squirrel on three sides, a three-walled jail about twenty centimeters high. He observed the creature coolly: would it try to escape? They always tried. Then he began to pound.

The squirrel's ear flew off and its body jumped against the rear wall of books. Malocchio retrieved it. He whacked it again, and the tiny tail flew off. With several more hits, the tail lay in small pieces. The body was harder. A direct hit only flattened it a bit. A hit to one side sent it bouncing against a book wall. Once it flew over the wall, and he had to disentangle his long legs and go find it under his dusty dresser.

Almost immediately a pounding had begun from the apartment above his. It started so quickly, it was as if the tenant above had been standing poised with a broom handle. Now the thumping came through his ceiling furiously. Malocchio ignored it. He had almost finished. All that remained of the squirrel were slivers and chunks of wood. Malocchio whacked the floor a few more times for good measure. The floor was beat-up and scarred from his repeated attacks, and wood splinters lay everywhere, but he only smiled.

Malocchio shoved the books out of his way, under the bed. Something scurried out from underneath, but it was only a small rat. *A cousin*, he thought. *A good sign.* Now all was right with the world.

day five

Friday, 6 a.m.

Bonggg, bonggg, bonggg . . .

Although the unprotected cathedral stoop was likely
the most dangerous place she had ever slept, and although the unforgiving stone made her groan in her
sleep every time she turned over, Alma awoke feeling
cheerful. She'd had the most wonderful dream about
flying. But the bells! They must have rung throughout
the night, but she'd slept through them. How many was
it this time? She didn't count. Six, maybe, or seven or
eight. It seemed they'd been ringing forever.

It was daylight anyway, still early, and she wasn't the
least bit afraid. *Look at me*, she wanted to shout. *I
guarded the cathedral all night and kept it safe.* She was the
Great Adventurer after all. But there was no one to tell.
But, wait, what was this?

She examined the coat. It was a thin gray wool, soft-
ened with age, like the one she wore in her flying dream

last night. How strange. She tried it on; it was shapeless and hung to her knees. The arms were too long; she rolled them up over her wrists. It had the feeling of a man's short work coat, but with no particular style. It smelled old, like the streets, like soot and car exhaust, but it was a tolerable smell, even oddly comforting. The morning was chilly, and she was glad to have it.

She tried the pockets, but they were empty. No, rather, at the very bottom of one was something. A piece of wood, a short, fat stick five or six centimeters long, two or three across. It was old wood, jagged at one end where it had broken off from a branch and smooth at the other. No longer green, but not rotten, either. Solid. It made her think of her little bird with a pang; she wouldn't leave it alone again. She put the wood back in her coat pocket for good luck. Today would be a good day, she thought. She didn't care that the sky was overcast and the air heavy.

Since the cathedral was still closed, Alma made her way to a park with a public restroom. There was no attendant to ask her for money, and the door was wide open. All the stalls but one required a coin, and that one was occupied. Alma waited until a scruffy, groggy older woman emerged.

Presently Alma copied the old woman at the sink, washing her face and hands and neck. The water was cold, and the paper towels stacked on the counter only seemed to smear the wet over her face, but Alma didn't mind.

She posed for her reflection in the mirror. With her cheeks shining and the funny, oversized coat with the rolled-up sleeves, she looked less like a skinny little girl and more like a real adventurer. Or a fighter. She lifted her arms: or a giant bird. If she could be anything at all, she would be a great eagle, flying over the world. She grinned at herself, and ran through the park, her new gray coat flapping around her. Men were sleeping on benches inside ratty old sleeping bags. *Lazybones,* she thought cheerfully. She leaped to touch branches hanging over the path. The day was made for running and jumping. For flying. On a day like today, anything seemed possible.

6:15 a.m.

For everyone but Gabi, breakfast at Madame Jouet's was a solemn affair. Payah kept her bespectacled eyes on her cereal bowl. She hunched so far over it that Madame asked whether she could see her food. Did Payah perhaps need her prescription changed? Payah shook her head.

"Then sit up straight, dear."

Hannah and Roc barely said a word, and Madame Jouet's usual morning chatter was forced.

"Madame—" Hannah began once. But Roc kicked her under the table.

Gabi bounced in his chair as always. His face shined, his curly red hair flew in all directions. "Can I open my presents now?"

"After school, Gabi. Tonight." Madame Jouet ruffled his hair fondly, and then absently rubbed her neck. She loved them all so much it made her throat hurt. *Where were the others?*

She fussed over their jackets, repeatedly counting. Ten hooks, four children, multiple jackets and sweaters hanging from each of the ten hooks. It was going to rain today, she was sure of it. Couldn't they feel it in the air? Why didn't they have more raincoats? She was sure there had been seven last week. Why did children grow so fast? Where was Gabi's little slicker, hadn't he hung it up properly?

On the way to school, Gabi ran ahead, then back, herding the other three along the sidewalk like a pup. Payah trudged behind Hannah and Roc, as if reluctant to go.

"I thought they might come back in the night," Hannah said with a sigh. "I was hoping."

Suddenly Roc stopped. "I'm not going to school."

Payah ran up beside him and grabbed his hand. "Me, neither."

"But you have to, Payah!" Hannah said sternly. "You're so little, they'll call Madame right away."

"Yeah," Roc agreed. "You and Gabi have to go."

"I'm not going if you're not."

Roc looked to Hannah for help. She shook her head; she knew what he was thinking. If the others were in danger, every moment was precious.

Gabi skidded to a stop next to them with a happy shout. "Are you talking about me?"

"After recess, then," Roc said to Hannah. "After Gabi's party."

Hannah agreed. "We'll all go."

"My party! My name day party!" Gabi raced away.

"We've got to stick together," Hannah said firmly. Payah reached for her hand and walked safely between the older two the rest of the way to school.

9 a.m.

For the first time in his life, Barlach overslept. He woke up deeply refreshed, as if he had been lying by a lake in the warm sun for hours, watching the ducks float and dive.

Without thinking, he made his narrow bed, straightened his already tidy room, gathered up a few wood chips he'd missed last night in the poor light, and ate a stale roll. He didn't make a lunch, for he was not going to work. He stood suddenly, surprised at himself. And yet he realized he had known this since he awoke. He didn't ponder what would happen if he skipped work. He'd never done it before. He smiled the tiniest ghost of a smile. How strange he felt.

He had no plan, but he knew there was one. It was like a map about to unfold before him. He simply had to keep going, and he would find out when he got there.

Once astride his bicycle, Barlach knew he was going

to the cathedral. It was as if he were being pulled there by a string. All right. He knew the way. Perhaps all the other times he had ridden by the cathedral had been in preparation for this day. But Barlach did not think about such things. He merely focused on the next step with the single-mindedness he had given to everything in his life.

It had something to do with the cathedral, and the girl. It had something to do, too, with why he spent hours carving little animals, to release them from the wood and set them free in the city.

Barlach knew these things in the blind, unthinking way a dog knows it's hungry. But he didn't worry over them. He only thought how cold he was without his coat.

9:45 a.m.

Inside the cathedral, someone was playing the organ again. The sound seemed to come from a long way away and all around at the same time. It pricked the skin. It was dark, eerie music that fit with the gray day. To Alma it hinted of graveyards in the mist and sailors slinking around wharves at night with knives in their teeth and murder in their hearts. She shivered. She had goose bumps even in this coat. Did the cathedral seem gloomy today because outside was gray and foreboding, or had it always been this way, only yesterday she hadn't noticed?

The music stopped. Alma rubbed a bare foot against her leg to warm it. The echoes went on and on within the building. But when they finally stopped, it seemed to her the gloom faded away with it. At least a little. The silence gave her a boost of courage, and she headed for her new home in the little chapel.

There was no one around, and she slipped over the railing and behind the table unseen. It was dimmer in here than before, with little light brightening the chapel through the stained glass windows and even less light making its way through the white cloth that served as her four walls. She lifted the cloth and scooted inside. There was her little bird. She held it to her cheek and stroked its feathers. She would never let it out of her possession again.

But look! she said to it. *Look what I've brought to keep you company.* She emptied her pockets of the treasures she had found this morning: a coin, a piece of wire, a matchbook with two matches left, a button, a rubber band, and the piece of wood she'd started with. She didn't know what she'd use any of her treasures for, if anything, but her little bird needed some friends. She lined them up in a row with great satisfaction.

We are robbers, you and I, she thought, switching the game. *This is our loot. We steal from the rich and give to the poor, like Robin Hood. You'll come on my next adventure, which will be . . . when we hold up a carriage of wealthy aristocrats.* She didn't know what aristocrats were, but she knew they were rich. Then suddenly she found herself again in the sultan's palace, having to choose which were the truly worthy gifts for the king. *The other travelers have all chosen gold and silver—but they were wrong!* she explained to the bird. As a result, they had been beheaded, or devoured by monsters. *We must choose useful, simple gifts—*

From the other side of the chancel echoed the announcement of the first tour. That meant it was ten o'clock. One of the first things Alma had done this morning was to read the signs in the cathedral. She learned when it opened and closed, and she saw that tours happened at ten, twelve, two, and four. Yes, there went the cathedral bell, not so loud as it sounded outside. One, two, three . . . she slid the bird into her coat pocket . . . ten bongs. As an afterthought, she grabbed the piece of wood as well.

When she imagined it safe, Alma slipped from her hiding place. She wanted to see the crypt again. That is, she felt like she had to, although in truth the idea filled her with dread. Something pulled at her, and if she were going to live here, she had to know what it was. She was both excited and scared, and she wanted to get it over with. Above all, she must not attract attention. She hung back near a young couple so that strangers might think she belonged to them. Ordinarily she might have examined them more closely; maybe she *could* go home with them. But not today. She had a home! She wrapped the coat tightly around her as if it could make her invisible.

Alma observed Malocchio. He was a giant stick figure of a man. Could he have been the one who gave her the jacket? Her secret guardian? The more she thought of it, the more likely it seemed. If so, she must find a way to thank him. She didn't want him to think her ungrateful. But she hesitated.

Just then, his glance fell upon Alma and lingered with obvious interest and a barely detectable flicker of something else, something she couldn't identify. She stood rooted to the stone floor, unable to take her eyes off him.

"If you'll all gather around," he began as before.

When he turned from her, Alma shuddered violently. She felt as cold and shivery as if someone had just emptied the stone birdbath down her back. Suddenly she longed for the sun. She wanted to run away from this quiet, solemn place to a haven of trees and wind and noisy birds. *But that's silly,* she chided herself. *I'm brave. I'm the Great Adventurer.* Besides, there wasn't any sun today. And she could only get into the crypt when he took her. She could go outside anytime.

The crypt pulled at her, and she gave in. But she hung back from the tour, following it at a distance. Still anxious to escape notice as much as possible, she abandoned the idea of trying to look like some couple's child in favor of more straightforward hiding. She kept to the shadows and stepped behind pillars to stay out of sight when she could. It was during one of these sideways steps that she bumped into the old man.

Barlach backed away with his hands before his face. It was an automatic gesture of protection, but it startled Alma. She jumped back.

"This is my pillar. Go away," she whispered. He was the same scruffy old man she'd seen yesterday. What was such a ruffian doing in a cathedral? Her cathedral.

Barlach made a garbled, inarticulate sound, as if he hadn't spoken in a long time.

"Go *on*. It's important. Go away!" Alma was not afraid of him now but merely annoyed, and stood her ground. She did not want Malocchio to see her as he pointed out the windows overhead. He hadn't seemed to notice her since the tour began.

"If you'll look up here, you'll see the Zodiac window. You probably can't read the inscription. No one can read Latin anymore. The French count refuses to surrender to the English, but a soldier—a traitor or a spy—dashes in, lifts the count's coat of mail, and stabs him."

Barlach seemed unable to move. His face was dark and shadowed, but Alma could see he was scowling. He didn't look at her.

"The count had already ordered this window built for the Virgin . . ." The tour moved off. Alma peered around the edge of the pillar to check. She glared at Barlach.

He gazed at her coat with a strange look. She pulled it closer. Was he cold? She had heard that old people get cold more easily. But she couldn't be bothered with an old crazy right now.

Still, he made her uneasy, staring at her like that. What did he want?

She slipped away from the pillar to follow the tour. She was a secret agent about to discover the men who were plotting to overthrow the government. Malocchio was their leader. The plotters were about to make their contact, and she must watch carefully.

When the tour passed behind the choir, along the

small hallway before the semicircular row of chapels, Alma caught herself humming nervously. A little girl picked up a candle from the candle tray. Her mother told her to put it back. "It's not yours."

"Whose is it?"

"I don't know. It belongs to the cathedral."

"Who does the cathedral belong to?"

Her mother shushed her.

But Malocchio had heard this last question. He leaned over the small child. "The cathedral belongs to him that cares for it." The child shrank behind her mother.

"What if your heart were torn out," Malocchio went on. "Would you still be loyal?" The mother gathered up her child in her arms. "I would. I would give my soul for this cathedral. That is the devotion it requires." Malocchio strode off at a brisk pace. Suddenly he stopped and turned back to the group, which hurried to catch up with him.

"What would you give your soul for, hmm?" But he didn't wait for an answer and strode away again.

Now and then Alma caught sight of the wretched old man hovering nearby. He didn't watch her, he was simply *there*. What was he doing here in her home? Why was he following her, if indeed he was. It was hard to tell, just as she hoped it was hard to tell that she was following the tour. She frowned at him when she could, but he didn't seem to notice.

When Malocchio started talking about the crypt, Alma couldn't help but listen. She'd heard the words before; this time she concentrated on his voice. What a voice. She would like to hear him sing. She covered her ears to block the words. Now she heard only a gentle up-and-down drone like a roller coaster in slow motion. It made her impatient: *Hurry up!* She tried to warm her toes on the back of her calf.

Her skin prickled at the idea of going into the crypt again. Yesterday she had thought it a deliciously eerie place, especially when she imagined ghosts floating on organ music and zombies lurking in shadows. On the other hand, something about the tour gave her butterflies in her stomach. Or was it Malocchio himself? What was it about him? What if he adopted her? Alma had been told she had a good head on her shoulders, if she would only grow up and use it. *Stop imagining things,* she'd been told a hundred times. She wondered if she were just imagining things now. How could she know?

Alma had just taken a step toward the others crowding at the crypt's door when a hand brushed her shoulder. It was rough and yet tentative, as if afraid of hurting her.

"No," a voice growled in her ear.

She swung around. It was the bent old man. His wrinkled face pulled back from hers, and under his overgrown eyebrows his eyes were wild and frightened.

Alma jerked away indignantly. She didn't like strangers to touch her, and she didn't like being told what to do, and besides that, the last thing she wanted was to draw attention to herself. She felt sorry for him, but still!

"Leave me alone," she hissed through clenched teeth.

Barlach anxiously watched the thin, angry figure disappear into the dark hole that led to some grimy underground mystery. He didn't know why he'd spoken to the girl, or why he felt such a horror of the crypt. It wasn't that he feared underground places; no place was better or worse than any other by itself. He might prefer the open streets to a crowded store, but he regularly cleaned out his landlady's basement, and he found it an acceptable space.

Nor did he fear the crypt itself. He had never seen one, but he knew what it was. No, it wasn't the crypt. What, then? Tortured as he had been over the years by his own fearsome imaginings—until he had managed to still them one by one and thus find some sort of empty peace—Barlach was peculiarly sensitive to shades and emanations of evil. He knew bad when he saw it.

The girl worried him. Something was very wrong

somewhere nearby, and it frightened him. For her. For some reason, he felt a vague, inarticulate yearning to protect her. Protect? He didn't call it that. He could not. After the terrible event years ago, he had weeded any such yearning from his heart. For himself he had no mercy: he had no right to protect anyone.

Nevertheless, with a great shudder, he followed her down the stairs.

In the crypt, the cold, dark air pressed against him. Barlach felt as though his presence were being resisted, but this was to be expected. He should not have been here. The tour guide spoke about the seamier history of the building—of politics, greed, and murder—while the tourists shuffled their feet and coughed nervously. His voice had a soothing, gentle drone. It made Barlach sleepy. He tried not to listen.

Alma wasn't listening, either. She had heard the stories before. Standing slightly behind the others, she slid unseen—she hoped—behind the old wooden door that stood open at the bottom of the stairs. She pressed herself against the cold wall and wished the others would hurry up and leave. Her pounding heart made such a racket that she could barely hear the guide's soft, mesmerizing voice. She concentrated on breathing quietly.

Only Barlach had noticed Alma. He hovered at the back of the crowd near the door like a faithful dog guarding its best friend. He had no plans and acted only on instinct. It was by instinct that, as the shadowy crowd shifted and pushed toward the grate in the middle of the floor, Barlach took a step sideways and found himself behind the door with Alma.

Alma held her breath, tense as any small creature confronted by an unexpected enemy in unknown territory.

Barlach twisted his already hunched body so that he, too, was hidden by the door, while keeping as much distance between himself and the girl as he could.

Alma thought hard. Should she make a run for it while she still could? But something paralyzed her. Fear? Or something else?

Finally, the guide ushered everyone out. The door banged hard behind him, and it was dark.

10:30 a.m.

It is never clear whether locked doors are meant to keep people in or out. In any case, the front gate of the city's schools was kept bolted until lunchtime, and opened only for visitors. But Hannah and Roc and the young ones were in a hurry. Gabi's party took place at midmorning recess, with much slapping of hands and spilling of punch. Just before it ended, Roc pulled Gabi aside and told him what to do. The two girls left the school yard one by one as if returning early to their classrooms, and minutes later all four slipped without notice through the school's back door.

"Where are we going?" asked Gabi. He had never skipped school before and was thrilled at this turn of events on his name day.

"We're going to look for the others," Roc said. He and Hannah had agreed that the less Gabi knew, the better. Gabi was too little and too talkative. Roc had wanted to leave him behind altogether, but what if they weren't back by lunch? Hannah pointed out that Gabi couldn't very well go home for lunch by himself.

"Where shall we start?" Hannah asked now.

"Let's just count our blessings and trust our intuition," Roc said, puffing out his cheeks and waddling in imitation of Madame Jouet. Gabi whooped in delight, Payah laughed unexpectedly, and even Hannah smiled.

"This way." Payah pointed toward the old part of the city. Hannah and Roc exchanged glances and followed her. It was spooky how often Payah just knew things. Gabi, as usual, lagged behind or raced ahead.

"I gotta go," he said to Roc breathlessly on one of his return trips. "For real this time."

"There's one near the cathedral," Roc said. They were only a block away.

Across the street from the cathedral stood an old-fashioned *pissoir*, its rounded iron walls rusty with age. "Go ahead," said Roc. "We'll meet you inside the cathedral."

"We should wait for him," Hannah said.

"It's only fifty meters away; what could happen? We'll be right there. Don't be such a worrywart."

"Race you," Payah yelled from the bottom of the cathedral steps. Roc ran after her. Hannah smiled to see Payah, always so serious, enjoying herself. It distracted her for the moment.

"I won!" Payah shouted from the top of the steps.

"Impossible!" Roc said. "You're too little."

Hannah caught up with them and Payah grabbed her hand.

Of the three children, only Payah had been inside the cathedral before. Madame Jouet took them to the neighborhood church—sometimes, when she thought of it. Madame Jouet's churchgoing depended upon the movement of the spirit within her, she told them, and often it moved her to sit in the park instead.

"I'll show you Jesus's hair!" Payah exclaimed, and led them to a reliquary box mounted in a wall. She showed them a spot where you could whisper and be heard across the building. She showed them engraved in a pillar a saint who had been decapitated and held his head under his arm. She showed them a sarcophagus with Saint George slaying the dragon.

"Where's Gabi?" Hannah asked suddenly. She and Roc looked at each other. How long had it been? Five minutes? Fifteen? "We should have waited for him!"

Immediately they headed for the door. "He should have found us by now," said Roc.

"We should have been paying more attention." Then she stopped. "Wait. Payah and I will look around in here. Maybe he's trying to find us."

While Roc searched outside, the two girls quickly walked through the cathedral, up one aisle and down the other. Gabi was not there.

Moments later, they joined Roc outside. He ran to meet them. "I went up and down the block."

Hannah tried to still her mounting fear. "He could have got distracted and wandered off. Met a friend or something."

Payah shook her head. Without a word, the three of them set off together to search the streets around the cathedral. The wind picked up. Clouds massed overhead, as if it might storm. There was no sign of a red-headed six-year-old.

"Where could he *be*?" cried Hannah.

"He's probably just hiding," Roc said. He sounded unconvinced.

"It's his name day," Payah reminded them.

"We should have warned him," said Hannah. "We should have told him what to look out for."

"Let's split up," Roc said. "You two go—"

"No!" cried Hannah. "From now on we have to stay together!"

"In there," Payah said suddenly, eyeing the cathedral. Hannah and Roc looked at each other and nodded.

10:45 a.m.

Alma sprang away from the hunched figure at the same moment that he stepped away from her, trying with a soft groan to straighten his bent back.

Barlach was sorry he was here. He wished for the comfort of his narrow bed—not much comfort after all, but in any case better than this. In his adult life it had not occurred to him to want a soft mattress or a feather pillow, and he wouldn't have permitted himself to own such a luxury if it had. But now a longing seized him. This dank, dark room was the coldest, emptiest place he had ever known, and he wished he had a soft blanket to wrap himself in.

Alma tried to think. She had wanted to explore the crypt alone, and now look! She was stuck down here with a crazy man. He didn't scare her exactly, but his presence disturbed her. She thought he was like someone in a fairy tale who had been turned into a monstrous beast because of offending a witch. But she could not afford to feel sympathy. She had to take care of herself. She edged farther away from him.

The room was empty, but its air was heavy and cold, and it pressed on her in a way that made it hard to breathe. What could have happened here in the past, Alma wondered. She hoped she wouldn't suffocate down here before anyone came back. Maybe she would grow roots like a tree, or turn to stone.

She shook herself. She'd come here for a reason. Moving, she discovered to her relief that she could move.

As her eyes grew accustomed to the dark, the glow from the hole in the center of the room seemed to grow stronger. It hadn't felt as bright before, when the overhead bulb was on. Now the soft yellow light floated up from beneath the grate like the ghost-light over a moor. Slowly Alma tiptoed toward it. There in the center lay the secret to the mystery, whatever it was. Beneath the bones might be a robber's treasure, or a magic ring, or a dragon's egg surrounded by fire. She would steal the egg and hatch it; she would like to ride on a dragon's back.

Carefully, so as not to make a sound, she lifted one

end of a section of guard fence and slowly swiveled it aside. She moved with excruciating slowness, averting her eyes from the hole itself. Now she dropped to her knees and flattened her body against the cold, bumpy stones. She could feel their indentations through her thin dress and the coat. She had just closed her eyes, briefly, imagining what she would see, when she heard a stirring behind her.

The old man. She had forgotten him for a moment. He was still hunched against the wall. Fiercely she waved at him to be still.

Now she peered cautiously past the edge of the floor into the hold below. A shudder passed through her. The spotlight showed the pile of old bones, a heap of skulls, ribs, what once must have been arms and legs. They were real. She hadn't imagined it yesterday. And she wasn't pretending now. The spotlight was not bright, but it created a pool of focus beyond which all was in shadow.

Wham! A door banged open beneath her. Lights came on.

Alma caught her breath.

"Go on, they won't hurt you. They're all sleeping."

It was the tour guide, leading a small boy with curly red hair, maybe six or seven years old. The boy looked around, and the man let go of his hand. Alma followed the boy's eyes, and only then did she notice for the first time, slumped against the wall directly beneath her, the row of children.

They sat on barrels or directly on the floor with their legs out in front of them. There were boys and girls both, between about six and twelve, she guessed. They looked like ordinary kids, maybe a little on the scruffy side, like they'd been out playing—like her, she thought. But they hadn't moved when the tour guide entered. They were sitting up, but they seemed to be sleeping. They reminded Alma suddenly of something she'd seen once at a fair—a row of people who'd agreed to be hypnotized. They did what they were told, pretending to drink water, scratching their armpits. One man had embraced a chair and tried to kiss it, making everyone laugh. The hypnotist said he could leave and they'd stay as he left them—all day if necessary—until he released them.

The little redheaded boy seemed to know some of the kids. He started toward them but stumbled and fell onto the pile of bones—or did the tour guide trip him? Frantically the boy squirmed off the pile. The bones clattered against each other. As if noticing the bones for the first time, the boy backed up, wide-eyed, away from them. He looked more impressed than afraid.

"Sit down," Malocchio said in his gentle voice.

The little boy looked to his friends for help, but no help was forthcoming. He glanced at the doorway.

"Don't be foolish. It's locked at the top. Sit down!"

With a defiant look, the boy slid to the ground. "I want to go back."

The tour guide sat on a barrel on the other side of the pile of bones. He took an open bottle of wine from atop a barrel next to him and poured himself a glass.

"I told you I had wonderful stories, and that is true. There are amazing things in this place, all manner of secrets and treasures." He took a sip. "Would you like a drink?"

The boy glared at him. "What stories? What treasures?"

"Do you know what the soul is, my boy?"

The boy didn't respond.

"But you've been baptized, have you not? You know your catechism?"

There was still no answer. Whatever enthusiasm the boy might have had for Malocchio's promises had evaporated. Malocchio sighed, and drank. He spoke softly. "You were taught about the soul, I suspect. But were you taught about the souls of glass and stone?" He took another sip. "Were you taught about the primacy of beauty? About what has a right to exist and what does not? Beauty is truth and truth beauty, and that is all you need to know."

Malocchio continued in this vein, speaking quietly. Alma felt herself drifting off, but a pinch on her foot brought her back. She didn't dare move but tried harder to block out the sound of the guide's gentle voice. She concentrated on the ungentle words.

"I love this place," he said now. "For twenty-five years I have been its sole guardian. Much is required of me to protect it, and not all of it is pleasant. This, here"—he gestured bitterly—"is the only kind of beauty that can be allowed to exist in the world. The kind that is permanent and fixed. Do you understand? If you were a painting . . . but you are not." He twirled his glass, gazing into it. "I have tolerated children, with your endless stupid questions, your interruptions, your . . . noise. But now"—his voice dropped—"that's not enough. They want someone who . . . *loves children.*" He seemed to choke on the words.

The boy's eyes were now closed, like the others'. When Alma's head began to droop, she felt another sharp pinch on her foot that jolted her awake.

"I wish there were another way," the man mused, taking another small sip. "But there isn't. If I can no longer remain here because of you—" In a sudden flash of rage, he hurled his glass against the opposite wall. Crash! It shattered on the stone. Alma flinched, but the children below didn't move. Malocchio stood up.

"I assure you your deaths will be painless, a tiny, necessary slaughter. I only await the sign that the right moment has come. I will know it when I see it. I believe it will be a girl, and she will be first. She will be delivered to me soon."

He took a final drink directly from the bottle, wiped the red drops from his lips, and recorked the bottle. "You will remain quiet now no matter what happens. No matter what you hear. You blend into the wall. You are invisible. I will return."

12:40 p.m.

It seemed like hours later when the next tour entered the crypt. Alma and Barlach slid unobtrusively from their hiding place behind the door and merged into the group. Trembling and deeply shaken, Alma avoided looking at Malocchio. Once upstairs, she made for the great west doors. Barlach trailed behind. He hadn't spoken a word since they'd entered the crypt.

Outside, working people on their lunch break, shoppers, travelers sat singly or in pairs on the cathedral steps, eating sandwiches and drinking juice out of triangular cartons or bottles. Heavy, dark clouds had gathered overhead since morning. Alma dropped weakly onto a step apart from other people. She kept one eye on the cathedral doors, ready to bolt if necessary, but she had to think. She was hungry, and tired, and she felt wrung out. She pulled the old coat more tightly around her.

Nearby, Barlach stood—desolate, waiting. Alma

turned on him fiercely, wiping her wet cheeks with the backs of her hands.

"Why are you following me?"

He croaked something indecipherable.

"Can't you talk?"

He cleared his throat. Alma noticed his pants were threadbare at the knees. It made her impatient. "You didn't hear any of it, did you?"

He looked at her blankly.

Alma's heart sank. Crazy as he was, he was a grownup. Maybe he could have helped. But he was useless. And what could she do alone? She was just a kid.

Barlach's jaw worked slowly. He shook his head. He rubbed his chest desperately; his heart hurt. "Why did you," he began, but his voice trailed away.

"What?" she insisted.

"The crypt," he said more slowly.

Couldn't he hurry? The tour guide could come out any minute!

"A bad place."

"Bad place? Ha!" Alma snorted. Her stomach was still in knots. What did he know?

"Why do you go down there?" It was Barlach's turn to insist. He peered into her face, listening hard.

"I don't know. Look, why—" Alma had never seen such a forlorn grown-up. "Why are you bothering me?" She needed real help, from someone strong and capable, like the person who had left her his coat, not like this helpless old man. "Go away."

Barlach wanted to go home. He pulled on his scraggly hair; he was almost beside himself with grief. He tried to think; the girl was so thin.

Alma watched him, struggled with herself, and then gave up. "He's going to *kill* them."

Barlach began to sway on his feet. He moaned softly.

Alma jumped up. "Hey! What—why don't you sit down? You can sit down."

He leaned on her arm, she was surprised at how lightly. She sat several feet away. He rested his head in his hands. She moved closer to him, to offer or receive comfort, she didn't know.

What could he say to this skinny, fierce little girl who reminded him vaguely of another child, a child who ran into the street after a pigeon, a child he hadn't actually seen until it was too late, the child whose memory he'd banished until now—the child he knew nothing about except what the mother had repeated over and over in her grief: *he loved animals.*

"It's dangerous," Barlach croaked now. "It can go out . . . so fast." How could he explain what he meant? How could he warn her?

But Alma didn't seem to hear. "It's too dark to see them when you're just looking at the bones," she mused. "If people could only *see.*"

Barlach watched her as if from a great distance. Her thin body trembled, rocked slightly within the old jacket, his jacket. For a moment she looked at him, and her eyes lost their customary defiance and seemed to plead with him to do something. But how could he help? He was old and useless. His heart twisted in his chest. It hurt.

Alma's own heart winced at the deep creases in the old man's face, the pain in his eyes, the anxious, sad droop of his head. "What can you do, then?" she cried.

Suddenly Barlach jerked as if an arrow had pierced him.

But it wasn't an arrow. It was a small stone, launched with careful aim by a child. It hit Barlach in the back, which seemed to be the signal for a band of wild banshees to attack.

1:10 p.m.

As if on signal, three children came leaping, shriek-ing with all their might down the steps toward Barlach. The other people on the steps looked on with annoy-ance or amusement, but Barlach reacted with terror. He clutched at his chest and fell backward.

Alma leaped up with a shrill cry. Something ex-ploded in her, like a firecracker in her head. She sprang in front of the old man, waving her arms at the intrud-ers and yelling her own earsplitting, raging battle yell. Whether she was screeching for herself or for the old man didn't matter. Without thinking, she plowed into the first of the attackers to reach her. It was Roc, and she hit him head-on. Together they bumped and rolled down the steps to the sidewalk.

The shrieking and yelling stopped. The other two children watched in shocked silence as the two tumbled down the steps. It was not at all what they had expected.

They clattered down after Roc and Alma. A few adults gathered around.

"Everybody all right?"

"A little rough, aren't you?"

"Shouldn't you be in school?"

Alma was embarrassed by the attention. She was indeed bruised and scraped, but she shrugged. But wait, this was the same boy—

"We're on a school trip," Roc said quickly.

The adults moved off.

Alma was pleased to see a lump starting to emerge on the boy's head. Yes, he and the older of the two girls with him were the same ones she had seen at the school. What was the girl's name? Hannah? But now they were in a hurry to leave. The younger girl tugged on the boy's hand.

"Come on, Roc."

"Wait!" Alma cried. "What'd you do that for?"

Roc drew himself up indignantly. "That's gratitude for you. We just saved your life. What a waste." He dusted himself off with exaggerated gestures.

"Saved my life?"

"From the kidnapper."

Alma whirled around. "Where?"

"Right next to you, ninny!"

What? Suddenly Alma understood. She looked around again, but the old man was gone. She faced the boy angrily. "The old man? Are you crazy? He's not a kidnapper! He's just a—a—"

"A what?" the younger girl asked, peering up from behind thick glasses.

"An old crazy, I guess. But you could have given him a heart attack, trying to scare him like that. He didn't do anything to you."

The older girl, Hannah, looked worried. But Roc was disgusted. "That's what we were *trying* to do." He stopped short of calling her an idiot.

"We didn't mean to hurt him," Hannah offered. "We just wanted to scare him away. We thought he might be—"

"Never mind," Roc said. "Let's go. We've got to find Gabi."

"He's lost," the little one offered, by way of parting. The three of them turned to go.

"Who's Gabi?" Alma called after them, though she thought she knew.

"He's one of—" Hannah hesitated, turning back. "He's our brother."

"Where'd he go?"

"He was kidnapped," the younger one said solemnly. Alma's heart sank. She could hardly speak.

"We don't know that for sure," Hannah said. "He could be hiding or something. Like the others. But they've disappeared."

"It's his name day," said the youngest.

Alma smiled in spite of herself. The little one was so earnest and serious. At that, Hannah asked her name and introduced herself and Roc. "And this is Payah."

"What kind of name is that?"

"*P.A. La Petite Aveugle.* Little Blind One. It's a nickname," Roc said, giving Payah a friendly punch. Payah watched Alma with interest.

"Did you go to the police?" Alma asked. Not that she would have, but she needed to know if policemen would be poking around.

"Of course not," said Roc.

"They might blame Madame," Hannah explained.

"She's like our mother," Payah said.

"She runs the shelter," Hannah said.

Living in a shelter and liking it? Alma didn't understand. But she had no time to ask them about it. "Look, I might—I saw—" But she stopped. What if she was wrong? What if it wasn't their Gabi? She could still just run away.

"What does he look like? Gabi." She glanced up at the cathedral. The main doors stood ajar—though she was sure they had been closed when she came out—and suddenly she felt as if a cold wind had swooped out and wrapped her with long, icy fingers, squeezing the breath out of her.

"Curly red hair, six years old," said Roc. "Little."

"Bouncy and smiley," said Payah.

"You've seen him!" said Hannah, following Alma's nervous glance. "In there?"

Dark clouds rumbled and whirled overhead. Alma pulled her coat around her. She tried to think, but her thoughts felt as thick as country mud. "I can't tell you here," she managed to say. "Let's go farther away. But hurry."

1:35 p.m.

Alma led the small party quickly to a tiny triangular park wedged between two streets that came together at an angle, a block from the cathedral. The cement-hard ground was strewn with flattened cigarette butts and bottle caps like fallen soldiers on a battlefield. Here and there a few sparse clumps of grass remained. The children squatted in a circle on the packed dirt.

"What is it?" Roc demanded. "Tell us now."

Alma wasn't sure how to begin. She didn't want to tell them she lived in the cathedral, it was too dangerous. But what could she say? *Face facts,* her social worker had said. *You're just a* gamine, *a lousy kid.* That was true—not a lousy kid, but a kid nonetheless, a Great Adventurer, yes, but eleven years old. What could she do in the face of real evil? But maybe with their help . . . She looked from face to face—Hannah worried, Roc irritable and impatient, Payah intently watching. She swallowed.

"There's this crypt." She told them how she had stayed in the crypt and what she had seen. When she got to the part about the other children sitting on barrels, Hannah interrupted her.

"What did they look like?"

Alma described them the best she could. The three others nodded to each other and ticked off their names one by one.

Alma told them the rest. They heard her out in silence.

"We have to go down there," Roc said when Alma finished.

"And then what?" Alma objected. "What could you do, the three of you? Even four?"

Roc said, "Not all of us. We can't all go, we have to be inconspicuous."

"We have to stay together," Hannah argued.

"We can't go down there when he's there," Roc said, "so we have to keep him occupied. You say there's a grate. What if one of us stayed below and slipped through it while the others made a commotion upstairs to keep him away?"

Distracted the monster himself? Slipped through the grate? "And then what?" Alma shook her head. "They're hypnotized, they won't move." Worse, Malocchio was everywhere, appearing silently like a snake when you least expected him. And what good would it do if they got caught? This she couldn't even mention.

They fell silent. Alma felt better to have told her new friends, but worse because they didn't know what to do. "Anyway," she said, "four is too many."

"Wait," Hannah said to Roc. "Maybe it would be okay if one of us goes with her while the others wait— you know, keep watch. All we want to do first is see if it's really them."

"I want to go," said Roc.

Alma didn't want to go down there again at all, whether the kids on the barrels were kids they knew or not. "You have to go down and stay after the tour leaves," she said doubtfully. "You can't see them otherwise. He does something with his voice. It's like he pulls down a curtain."

Payah spoke up for the first time. "It doesn't matter *who* it is down there."

They all looked at her. "Right, Payah," Hannah said, and hugged her.

Alma wondered what it would be like to be part of this family. "What's your real name?" she asked Payah.

"I don't know. I've always been called that."

"Her real name is Payah," Roc said.

"You could make up a name. Like Isabelle, or Diana, or Rubaiyat. Something bold and all your own. Any name you want."

Roc poked Payah gently in the side. "Payah is a good nickname. It means you're special."

Alma shook her head. Not having your right name was almost as bad as not having a home. Payah smiled at her gratefully. Roc plucked a rare blade of grass and blew a terrific shriek with it between his thumbs.

Hannah jumped up. "We've got to hurry!"

A loud but distant crack followed by rumbling thunder answered her. The others scrambled to their feet. Hannah said to Alma, over the rising wind, "Lead the way."

2:05 p.m.

Inside the cathedral a few minutes later, Alma spoke in a whisper.

"There's the tour. It's already started. Listen, Roc." She couldn't look him in the eye. "I think you should go by yourself. It'll be safer. But—" She sneaked a peek at his face, saw he was barely listening, watching the tour guide. Tall, thin, strangely bony, his skin pale against his dark clothes, the man seemed to sway before the little group assembled around him. Alma grabbed Roc's arm and shook him. "Listen to me! Don't look at his eyes, and don't listen to what he says. Stay with the group no matter what. And it helps to touch someone else—like their shirt or jacket or something."

Roc shook off her hand and drifted over to join the tour as planned.

The three girls waited in a pew close to the altar. It would take a long time for Roc to go down to the crypt, see what he needed to see, and wait for the four o'clock tour group to come down so he could sneak out with them. Alma would rather have waited outside in spite of the coming storm, but said they should stay here in case anything happened.

"What could happen?" Hannah asked in alarm.

Alma didn't answer. She only knew she needed to keep watch.

Next to Alma, Payah sat very still. The cathedral was bleak and dark. There were no shifting patches of color anywhere, no radiant statues half-alive, only cold gray stone. Alma felt chilled all through her in spite of her coat; she sat on her hands to try to warm them. The wooden pews were uncomfortably hard to sit on for long. She tucked her cold feet beneath her.

"How come you don't wear shoes?" Payah asked.

Alma shrugged. She wished she had her old brown shoes back. "I lost them. But look what I found." She showed Payah and Hannah the little bird.

"Oh!" said Hannah. "I found something like that once on a fence. It was a little bear cub. I still have it. And Payah found a little tiny cat on a statue in the park. Didn't you? They're at home."

After a while Payah put her head in Alma's lap and

fell asleep. Hannah smiled. Gently Alma pried the bird from Payah's hand and slid it back into her own pocket.

Then Alma started. "Something's wrong." Malocchio had reappeared—the tour must be over—but he was heading away from the chancel toward the south door, with an overcoat over his arm, as if he were leaving for the day.

Alma had no time to think. It was now or never. "Hannah!" she whispered. She let down Payah's head carefully onto the dark oak pew.

"What's the matter?"

"There must be no four o'clock tour today for some reason, and Roc is still down there. He can't stay there all night, something terrible will happen. And if he's leaving—Malocchio, I mean, the tour guide—this may be our only chance."

"You mean go down there now?"

Alma nodded.

"But I thought—"

"Come on!"

"Where are you going?" Payah had woken up.

"You stay here and wait," Hannah said. "But keep out of sight."

"I want to come with you!"

Alma hesitated. "She's too little. Maybe she— Maybe you and she— Maybe you should take her home and I'll go ahead."

"No!" Hannah and Payah said together. Several adult heads turned to look at them.

"Shh! Not so loud! Okay, let's go then."

"Oh no," cried Hannah. "There's that man again!"

2:10 p.m.

Barlach had been riding crazily, silently, through the crowded streets for some time, until finally his gnarled legs could pump the pedals no more. He slowed, stopped, oblivious of the traffic flowing around him like a stream around a stone. He pounded the handlebars. His face was lined and drawn. His head drooped as if he lacked the strength to hold it up.

Several minutes later, he lay on his back on a wooden bench under the darkening sky. He didn't notice when a teenaged boy slouched by, eyed the bicycle, which had never had a lock, ran his fingers along the worn seat, bent to examine the tires, shrugged, and without a second glance at Barlach—who in any case had his eyes closed and couldn't hear—hopped on and rode away. His triumphant whoop was lost in the wind and the traffic.

Almost an hour later, Barlach sat up stiffly and

rubbed his neck. He rubbed his thighs, which hurt, and his arms. He was cold. The temperature had dropped; a storm was coming. Where was his coat? Oh, yes, he remembered. He looked thoughtful. What was he doing here? Where was his bicycle, his trusty friend?

Never mind. Even that didn't matter now. He woke up knowing something he hadn't known before.

Barlach had not been the man he wanted to be. He was not brave, or strong, or heroic. He had not been the kind of man who would leap into a fire to rescue a child. Instead he had been frightened—all his life. But that was over now. He was calm. He had been given a second chance. It was like a puff of pollen on the wind, or a dandelion seed, floating and delicate—and that in itself was frightening: he might crush it, wreck it. But it had come to him nonetheless. To him. Barlach. He was ready.

He set off in the direction of the cathedral, on foot. His heart beat raggedly, but he didn't notice.

He thought of Alma lying on the crypt floor, peering into the strange hole. He thought of her hiding behind pillars, playing some sort of game, wearing his jacket loosely around her shoulders. He thought of her curled up, sleeping in front of the cathedral. He saw her tumbling down the cathedral steps, and his heart tightened; he should have . . . but no, it was too late, it was over. He remembered the way he first saw her, looking fierce and angry and scared, with her knees drawn up to her chest, clutching the edge of the pew, and he knew how she felt. She was like him and he wanted to help her. He didn't know how. He only knew that he must. His life—his very soul—depended on it.

2:45 p.m.

"All right, *madame*. That will be all."

Talking to the police had not been easy for Madame Jouet. She knew the risks. They could have said she was irresponsible and taken away the rest of her children or closed her place down. She ran the shelter only half officially anyway. The town council stayed out of her business and she stayed out of trouble. But the police were more worried about the missing children than about her. They were not politicians, they were men who had sworn to protect the citizens. They were fathers.

Perhaps she should have gone to them earlier. But how could she have known they'd treat her so well?

Madame Jouet glanced at the sky and pulled her bright shawl around her more tightly in the wind. Of course she had shuttered the ground floor's windows when she left, like any good French householder, but she wished she had thought to close the twelve windows upstairs.

Still, she felt better. She didn't expect they could help much, with only six *gendarmes* for the whole town, but at least they knew. It was her last hope. She could think of nothing else.

Madame Jouet had looked everywhere. This morning she had walked the streets again, looking desperately in every shop window and every alley. She returned to the street where Barlach had disappeared the day before, but found nothing. She walked from one end of town to the other. Her feet hurt. She realized she had half expected that the missing children would, after all, magically reappear for Gabi's sake. But they hadn't.

She leaned into the wind, pressing her red hat to her head with one hand to keep it from flying off, holding on to her striped shawl with the other. Her colorful skirts caught the wind and made walking hard work. Since she was tired and could think of nothing else to do, she would go to the cathedral. She'd never been much of one for prayer, but if she were going to pray, she might as well do it in the sort of place God might listen, if He listened at all. He didn't seem to have been paying much attention to the prayers she had uttered from her kitchen during the past few days. She wasn't sure she believed in God, anyway, but *something* made people want to build beautiful places. Perhaps she had been remiss in never taking her children to the cathedral. She'd simply never thought of it, having been there only a few times herself. If they all came back to her alive and well, she would pack them up and take them there.

Useless, irresponsible woman, Madame Jouet berated herself. And she hurried to do one more desperately loving, useless thing on behalf of her children.

3:05 p.m.

"There he is," Hannah whispered again.

Barlach hovered uncertainly, on unsteady legs, at the back of the cathedral.

"Now what? We need to get rid of him."

"No!" Alma almost shouted. "He's all right," she amended, seeing the surprise in their faces.

"So you do know him," Hannah said. It wasn't an accusation, only her usual need for accuracy.

Alma hesitated. She didn't exactly *know* him, but they had been in the crypt together, and they had talked, sort of. If you could call that talking. She looked back over her shoulder, but the old man had disappeared into the shadows. Alma started to explain, but Payah interrupted her with a cry.

"*Maman!*" She scrambled out of the pew. Hannah groaned.

"It's Madame Jouet," Hannah explained to Alma, who had sat up in the pew at the sight of the woman in the red hat who had eyed her so intensely yesterday. Who was she? "She'll want to know why we're not in school. She hates us to miss it. I've got to go."

"But we have to hurry. Roc—"

"Not for good. But she'll mess things up, believe me! I have to get her away. You go get him, okay?"

Alma couldn't look at Hannah. Instead she watched Payah hugging Madame Jouet through her colorful skirts.

"Meet us outside, okay? We'll wait for you." And Hannah was gone.

Alma didn't want to go down to the crypt again—and especially by herself. She wanted to walk out the door and leave Roc and all the rest of them. She thought about sneaking away to her hideout and waiting there until it was all over, whatever it was. But Malocchio was going to *kill* them. She had to help, even if she lost the one home she'd ever found for herself. She touched the little bird in her pocket for courage.

With a quick look around, Alma slipped into the shadows of a side aisle. The increasing dark outside made it even darker in the cathedral. In the dim light, the stone saints on the columns looked grim and forbidding. They offered no comfort. What did she expect? Then she saw Barlach, leaning wearily against a wooden railing, watching her. She hurried toward him.

"You came back."

Barlach reached out to touch her coat. Alma drew back, and yet—something in the old man's face made her wonder. *Could it be?*

"Don't sleep outside," he growled, jolting her back to the present.

"I don't! Not usually." She glared at him. What did he think she was, some sort of street urchin? "I have a home." She lifted her chin proudly. "Here."

He peered at her, trying to hear. "This is not a bad place—for a priest, or a bird." Outside, the thunder rolled slowly closer. "Up there." He waved his gnarled hand toward the ceiling. "Not—not under the ground like a . . . like a . . ." He shuddered as if wracked with sudden pain, and then the spasm passed. He glanced at Alma in short, furtive bursts, and otherwise kept his eyes on the floor, or upon her coat.

"I wish I *were* a bird," Alma said, pushing up one of

the sleeves that had come unrolled. "I'd stay here forever." Suddenly she felt shy. Why was she saying such
things to him, of all people? How was it that he, this
crumpled old *clochard,* made her feel brave?

"I'll be right back," she said. "Someone is in trouble." She remembered the morning and her nervous-
ness made her speak more sharply. "But you can't come
with me. I have to do this by myself."

Barlach's bent body strained after Alma like a dog
told to stay but longing to follow. He watched her hurry
toward the altar area and disappear behind it, and felt as
though his heart would break. He listened anxiously for
some sound to tell where she had gone, but his ears
were too old.

The small wooden door in the south transept
opened, and Malocchio entered the building. He
scanned the nave, scowling, and then strode across the
stone floor to the altar. His stubbly colorless hair stood
on end and his face was as pale as if he were devouring
himself from within.

Barlach shuddered when he saw the tour guide.
Something about the thin man made Barlach's old dry
skin crawl, even more now than it had outside the crypt.

The guide looked to Barlach like an angry demon, burning up with cold fire. What did he want? It was his eyes, yellowish gray. Was he sick, or mad?

Alma was in peril. Barlach knew this for sure, though he couldn't have said how he knew. Slowly, on twisted legs that ached from walking long blocks he usually rode, he followed Malocchio. Malocchio crossed the nave to the half-disguised wooden door in the base of the raised podium.

3:13 p.m.

Alma had no idea what she was going to do once she got to the crypt. She just knew she had to go. Everything in her wanted to stay above ground where it was light and open. Her legs felt heavier with every step. But no one saw her edge behind the choir or open the heavy door that led down to the crypt and pull it shut behind her.

Inside, the staircase was even darker and more cheerless than she remembered. Malocchio had turned on a light for them before, but she didn't know where it was. The hairs on the back of her neck stood on end. After a long moment her eyes adjusted to the dark and she saw a tiny bar of light coming from underneath the door at the bottom of the stairs—the door she had hidden behind earlier. She took a deep breath and started down.

At the bottom she pushed open the door. "Roc?" Her voice came out in a croak. He was huddled in the corner beyond the grate, just inside the barrier, completely still. He didn't answer. She whispered more loudly a second time.

"It's them," he said finally. "Gabi and the others." He recited their names in a strange voice, as if reading the names of the dead at school on *le jour de l'Armistice*.

Alma moved aside the steel fence, unconcerned about noise this time. She dropped beside him. Leaning over the edge, she could see into the shadowed corners below. Quiet children lined one side of the room, with the pile of bones in the center. They looked stiff and saggy at the same time; the ones on the floor sat with their legs straight out like plastic dolls whose limbs didn't bend. Five of the ten turned their heads toward her, toward Roc, but their faces were blank.

"It's like they can hear me but can't react," Roc said.

"Zombie-kids," Alma agreed.

Roc said nothing. He stared at them as if he couldn't think of what to do next.

"Let's see if we can get down there," Alma said.

"Yeah. Yeah, okay."

She didn't know what they were going to do, either, but whatever it was, they had to do it fast and get out of there. The low ceiling and heavy stone walls felt like they were closing in on her. She longed to be above ground where she could breathe.

The bars of the grate were spaced widely enough apart for Alma to squeeze through, head and shoulders first, then the rest of her. She gripped the bars and dropped to the packed earth floor not far below. Roc followed.

The children that Roc knew watched him with unexpressive eyes. The others remained oblivious, or asleep. Either they didn't hear him, or they were too far gone to care.

"We can't carry them. We have to wake them up," Roc whispered.

Alma nodded. But how were they going to do that? She didn't even know them. She took a deep breath and imagined herself the big sister in a family of zombie-kids, who looked up to her and needed her help. She was the Queen of Sisters, Sister Queen of the World. Her siblings had a terrible disease and only she could save them. She and Roc. Okay. She stepped up to the first child, a little boy dressed in shorts and an oversized T-shirt, barefoot like herself, and gently patted his feet. They were icy cold. She rubbed his chilly feet until they felt warmer, and then his hands. She brushed his pale cheeks with her fingertips. Quietly she moved from child to child, touching each one, patting them, trying to warm them up. One older boy had torn jeans and long curly hair falling over his forehead. A little girl with dark spiky hair had on pink overalls with a bunny on the front.

Roc watched Alma and then did the same, starting with Gabi. He tried snapping his fingers before Gabi's face, and slapped lightly at his legs and shoulders. He called his name over and over. He shook him. But nothing happened.

Suddenly the room grew cold. Alma and Roc stopped abruptly, mid-motion. Slowly the zombie-children raised their heads. Alma wheeled around.

She was greeted by soft laughter.

3:19 p.m.

"You see how it is? Everything takes patience. I waited for a sign, and a sign has arrived. How good of you to come." He addressed Alma now. "How kind, to save me the effort of having to run after you. It puzzled me that you had eluded me thus far, but now I understand why. I only had to wait. You are the final sign that it is time."

Malocchio stood framed in a shadowy doorway she hadn't noticed before. It was barely more than a dark hole in the wall, with a wooden door that had swung open on silent hinges. Roc took a step away from Alma. Alma's heart thrashed in her chest like a bird trapped under a box.

"And since at least one of you is immune to my charms, we will have some fun. The old-fashioned way. A game of cat and mouse, in which I am the cat."

Malocchio moved into the chamber so slowly they

hardly noticed. He inched, oozed, rather than walked. Between him and the two children lay the circular pile of bones almost a meter high and over a meter wide. Roc and Alma moved farther apart so they stood more toward the corners, equidistant from the tour guide. The man glanced slyly from Roc to Alma and back—and then he lunged at Alma.

Alma leaped out of Malocchio's reach. She grabbed a bone from the pile and heaved it at him as hard as she could. Malocchio turned and the bone glanced off his shoulder. Roc had picked up a long bone, too, and held it like a weapon.

Malocchio laughed. "Good, good. Go down fighting. Fight to the death. It disguises sorrow and whets the appetite."

Alma didn't move. In a split second she saw that their positions had shifted. Although she was stuck in a back corner, Roc was almost as close to the doorway as Malocchio. If she could draw Malocchio two steps closer to her, Roc could escape. But Malocchio looked steadily at Roc. To get his attention Alma yelled—shrieked like a hawk in distress.

Roc jumped at the sound. Malocchio barely glanced

at Alma and then grabbed at Roc, who sprang to the right, still wielding his long bone like a sword. Now the way to the door was clear. Alma saw her chance; she dashed to the doorway. She had to get air and light. She had to go up.

Suddenly before her appeared a figure out of nowhere. He almost collided with Alma. In her surprise, she almost didn't recognize him. The old *clochard* who had seemed so frail before, worn out and useless as an old sack, had in a matter of seconds gathered force and bulk. He filled the doorway like a great bear. Now he shifted his weight to one side and Alma darted past him into the dark corridor beyond. His crooked hand brushed her shoulder and gave her courage.

Malocchio snarled, as if sensing a true enemy for the first time. He rushed at Barlach in fury and tried to shove him out of the way. But Barlach resisted. With a scorching rage of his own and all the stubbornness of his years of solitude, Barlach stood his ground. It took many long seconds for Malocchio to dislodge the old man from the doorway, and Alma ran like the wind.

Malocchio took off down the tunnel after her.

Roc paused long enough to help Barlach to his feet.

The two eyed each other with a puzzled acceptance, neither one understanding why the other was there. Barlach nodded and the boy was gone.

Stiffly, Barlach followed, though his joints burned and his muscles ached and his heart knocked in his chest with a strange, irregular knocking. He ignored it. He felt more alive than he had ever felt. He felt . . . happy.

He had to go on.

Alma ran down the dark corridor as fast as she dared, hoping she wouldn't pitch headlong into a wall. In the dark she tripped hard. Pain shot up her leg and she fell forward, scraping her hands. But she felt the stairs. She scrambled up them like a monkey on all fours. Malocchio—for she knew it was he—came hissing, breathing hard behind her.

When she felt the door at the top, she hurled her weight against it and it swung open.

Where was she? She blinked fast. In the cathedral, yes, but where? She got her bearings—she was under the priest's podium—and ran. She had no plan, she only followed her instincts. Up. She had to go up.

She raced down the side aisle of the empty cathedral.

She didn't know where she was going. She had to get away, and she wanted to draw Malocchio away from the crypt. She ran for her life. She didn't notice Madame Jouet and Payah and Hannah across the nave or hear Hannah's exclamation of surprise and fear. She no longer heard the footsteps of the others as they ran after her. She didn't notice the clatter of the metal stanchion in front of the bell tower entrance as she knocked it over in her haste. She was aware now only of her own body in motion. Up the winding steps she sped. This time there was no one around to stop her. She ran effortlessly, urged on by her fear and her great impulse to climb, to take flight.

Alma was light on her feet but small. Malocchio's legs were much longer. Now she heard him as he entered the bell tower behind her, panting harshly. Within the cramped stone stairwell, his heavy steps pounded behind her. And behind him, in a jumble of footsteps and cries, came Roc, Barlach, Hannah, Payah, and finally, Madame Jouet.

3:27 p.m.

Madame Jouet charged up the narrow, winding stone stairway inside the bell tower, too frightened and distracted even to count the steps or notice she had lost her favorite red hat. The way was lit by tiny shafts of gray light through narrow slits in the walls, built for archers hundreds of years ago. Outside, the wind blew harder, driving the thunder before it. It came in earsplitting cracks and rumbles. Ahead of her the children began shouting.

Hatless and puffing, she reached a landing where a heavy rope hung down through a large hole overhead. Against the opposite wall, a wooden ladder led upward. She hesitated only a second, and in that instant heard a raspy breath being drawn.

She didn't see him at first. He was hunched against the opposite wall, clutching his chest. It was he. She'd thought so when she glimpsed him across the cathedral. But how could it be? The one who rode his bicycle all the time. *Le Fou*.

She observed him bent nearly to the floor and her heart didn't constrict as it usually did at the sight of him. He looked more like an old man who needed help than like a monster. An old beaten dog. She didn't know what he might have done in the past, and she might never know, but suddenly she was certain that he meant her children no harm.

These thoughts flew through Madame's mind in the small seconds it took her to cross the platform to the ladder. She had an urge to make sure he was all right— but she couldn't help him now. There was no time. The children needed her. She climbed the ladder.

Barlach never looked up. He didn't see or hear Madame Jouet. His head had sunk onto his chest in despair. His heart called out, but his legs would not move anymore. He had crawled the last few steps; he could not go any farther. He would have to give up. He could not save the girl.

Madame scrambled over the top of the ladder to reach the tower's upper landing. The cathedral's great bronze bell hung in the center of an airy, vaulted room open to the elements. Its rope fell through a hole to the landing below. Through the tall, stone, arched window openings, the wind rushed in and out. There were no workmen anywhere; they were taking a break.

Madame Jouet gasped. Payah stood at one of the arched openings. Beyond her, outside on the scaffolding, stood Hannah and Roc. Madame Jouet was at the window in a bound.

Now she saw it all. Outside, hundreds of feet above the slate and terra-cotta roofs below, supported by only a few narrow planks of wood and some thin iron scaffolding, stood the children: Roc, Hannah, and the little waif she'd seen yesterday. They were all her children now. And between the thin girl and the other two was the devil himself—a tall, bony rodent of a man whose gray face was contorted into a furious mask. He leaned precariously toward the girl like a rat about to bite.

3:29 p.m.

The children had stopped shouting. For a brief second no one moved. Around them raged a gale wind, hurling black clouds about overhead. Jagged lightning cracked the sky, and out of those cracks rolled great crashing boulders of thunder. Payah held on to Madame Jouet with both arms.

The scaffolding only reached around three sides of the tower; wooden planking jutted precipitously over the iron frame at one end. Alma had climbed from the tower out onto the scaffolding without thinking, and without thinking she had climbed over the iron bars onto the unprotected planks—two narrow boards placed side by side. Taut and red-cheeked, she edged closer to the end of the planks. Her oversized coat flapped in the wind. There was nothing directly beneath her, only the sidewalk, miles away.

Her legs felt like rubber. She was not afraid of high

places, but she stood outside the scaffolding now, and there was nothing to hold on to, nothing she could reach. If she fell, she would not fly like a bird in spite of all her pretending. She would simply fall like a stone. Still she would rather die here than below in the crypt. The scaffolding jiggled and she trembled, but she stood up straighter.

Barely a meter away, Malocchio clutched the scaffolding. He was breathing hard, and his wide, desperate eyes were fixed on Alma. When he moved, the planks wobbled like the slats of a suspension bridge, and the entire scaffolding swayed—and he held on more tightly. With a grimace he began to inch toward her.

3:31 p.m.

One floor below, inside the bell tower, Barlach sensed the struggle above him as clearly as if it were taking place inside his own skull. He saw Malocchio, gaunt and mean as a starving rodent, chasing Alma across the nave. He saw Alma flying before him, a little sparrow whose life was in danger.

He had no strength left. But he remembered Alma on the cathedral steps, looking at him with her head cocked, inquisitive and fierce, and he struggled to his feet. He reached overhead and managed to loop both hands around the heavy rope that rang the great bell. With one last colossal effort, as if nothing else mattered in the world, he pulled. In the vaulted room overhead, the great bell began to sway. With all the weight of his bent, weakened body, he pulled harder.

Abruptly the wind died around the bell tower. In the distance, a single bird screeched a warning.

Again and again, with his last strength, Barlach pulled on the rope. And the great bell rang.

It was not the recorded sound usually played on the hour, but a fierce, throat-constricting, earsplitting clang. Barlach rang the bell again and again, even though his heart felt as though it were about to burst. He rang the bell with all his heart and all his might, and its fierce, angry roar stopped passersby in their tracks. It shook the cathedral to its core.

3:32 p.m.

The wind stopped. It was as if the whole world stopped. There came a moment of stillness. The sound rolled out of the tower in great waves and almost knocked Madame Jouet off her feet. The bell rang and rang.

And then, as abruptly as it had stopped, the wind whipped up again. The world came alive. Madame Jouet shouted at Malocchio. Payah, peering around Madame's skirts, yelled at Hannah and Roc. And just as Hannah and Roc were about to leap at Malocchio, the skies opened with a great crack, and a heavy rain lashed them all.

Alma stood straight and spread her arms wide. What a place. It was so beautiful—the dark clouds overhead blending to mottled gray, the magnificent stonework all around her, the sienna and dun-colored roofs of the city below, and the bell, pealing, sending out those great waves of sound. She could imagine riding across the sky on them like a warrior on a chariot. The rain drenched her hair and face, but she didn't notice. Her fear fell away, and her uncertainty: she was indeed the Great Adventurer, a queen of this tower, at home in the air, a golden eagle that glided over cities. A great joy swelled inside her. The old gray coat protected her from the worst of the rain, and she spread her arms wide.

But Hannah and Roc dropped instinctively to all fours, clutching the edges of the planks so as not to be blown off. With a shudder, Malocchio lunged for the scaffolding behind him, and the planking shook violently. He cringed and shook and reached for a stone gargoyle for more support. The stone creature seemed to leer at him. Malocchio shivered—and noticed Hannah and Roc for the first time. His eyes narrowed. He glanced back at Alma and at the distance below.

He'd spent his life in the service of the cathedral. He'd spent many hours doing research and read hundreds of articles. He'd pored over his books, studying and learning everything he could, every legend, every piece of history. He'd examined dozens of stone carvings from every angle and kept them free of dust and dirt. He'd saved the side chapels where the beautiful paintings hung by blocking them off so tourists had to lean in over the railings. He'd wiped down those same iron railings that children's sticky hands might have touched. He'd tried to protect the cathedral from people, especially children. He tried finally to keep children out altogether, but the bishop had objected.

And now it was he who would be banished.

The rain stung his face like a hundred tiny arrows of fire.

He looked around him now. What was he doing up here in this horrible storm with these children? He'd lied when he said he loved children. He hated children. With all his heart and all his might. His feelings went beyond words. They were worse than those miserable little wooden figures he found around the city. They had no right to be here. No right.

Now it didn't matter to him which child went first. They all had to go.

Alma caught glimpses of Malocchio's face as he cowered before the storm. She saw it contort with such malice it made her tremble.

Bonggg, bonggg came the bell. Insistent, urging.

Malocchio eyed them now with feverish desperation—the wild girl alone at the edge of the plank and the pair inside, clinging to the boards and each other—and then he seemed to make up his mind. Eyes blazing, thin body trembling and soaked, his face contracted against the pelting rain, he finally turned from Alma. His weight shifted, and he swung a leg back over the horizontal pole of the scaffolding toward Hannah and Roc.

Alma gasped. He was going after her friends!

An unholy anger exploded within her, a burst of heat in her chest that she felt all the way to the back of her neck and the soles of her feet. The tips of her fingers burned. She didn't think. She gathered her strength, pulling her coat close around her, and in the next second, before Malocchio had completed his climb over the scaffolding, she bounced hard on the boards.

Malocchio turned back to her, his eyes wide with surprise. At the sight of her, wild and fierce, undaunted, defiant, his soaked bony figure seemed to balloon with its own outrage. Who was this child who threatened his cathedral, his world? This thin, scrawny wretch of a child with shining eyes? With a hiss, he released the scaffolding and lurched toward her, his arms outstretched.

Alma could not back up any farther. In a split second, between half-closed eyes, she saw, behind Malocchio, Hannah and Roc still crouched within the scaffolding, their faces full of terror. She knew they were afraid to move lest they cause her to fall. For a fleeting instant, she imagined falling to her death and never seeing her new friends again.

No. She was a mighty warrior. A warrior queen. The Great Explorer, with a band of fellow explorers—Hannah and Roc and little Payah. Warriors together.

The bell rang on.

When Malocchio lurched toward her, Alma knew she couldn't back up any farther. But the sound of the bell enveloped her like great protective arms. With all the strength she possessed, she bounced again.

The planks were slick with rain. The bounce sent her higher into the air than anyone. There was a good chance she would slip and fall. But she was as agile as she was determined, and she didn't.

Malocchio reached for her at that moment. He made a final, desperate grab. But as Alma jumped, the board buckled. The jolt thrust Malocchio into the air. It was only a few centimeters, but it frightened him. He staggered and jerked sideways to right himself. The boards shook beneath his frantically shifting weight. He arched backward in an almost inhuman effort to regain his footing. But it was too late. Clutching wildly at the air, twisting toward the cathedral one last time, his body writhing like one of the souls falling into hell carved over the cathedral's great entrance, Malocchio fell.

A furious howl trailed behind him and dissolved on the wind.

3:35 p.m.

Hannah and Roc stared in horror. They gripped one another, buffeted by sheets of rain. The last echoes of the great bell faded away. The thunder moved off as quickly as it had come; the rain fell more gently now. Alma climbed back over the scaffolding, and they gave her a hand. Quietly the three of them looked out over the town, their hair and clothes streaming.

"Well," Alma said. She didn't know whether to laugh or cry.

"*Venez, venez,*" urged Madame Jouet. "Come on!" The three children climbed back inside the bell tower, and Alma had only a second to hesitate before Madame Jouet enfolded her in her arms. Payah hugged her at the same time from behind. They all spoke at once.

"*Mon Dieu, mon Dieu*, what a terrible accident," fussed Madame.

"What happened? What did you do?" asked Payah.

"I can't believe it," said Roc.

"Let's get out of here," said Hannah.

"You poor dears, you're freezing to death, we've got to get you home, what madness, I can't imagine . . ." Madame went on and on.

"I didn't exactly mean—" Alma started.

"Shh, shh," said Madame. "Plenty of time for that later. Now you need some dry clothes, a hot bath—" She herded them down the ladder, still murmuring and fussing.

Alma saw Barlach when she reached the floor below. "Wait," she said. "I mean, go on. I'll be there in a second." Hannah hugged her briefly, and looked over her shoulder to see Alma bent over the old man.

Barlach lay still, his creased face relaxed. One fist was entwined in the thick rope. Alma touched his wild eyebrows lightly with one finger. Poor old man. Who was he? What had his life been? He was like a fallen warrior, but there was no one to carry him through the streets or make up a ballad praising his brave deeds. If he'd ever done any. Strange old *clochard*. But he had come to save her in the crypt, and he had rung the bell— for her. His courage had become hers. She didn't know how, or why, but she knew it was so. It was a mystery.

Curled up in a ball, he looked so cold. She took off her coat and knelt beside him. It was dripping wet on the outside, but still dry on the inside. She draped it over him.

"Goodbye, old man. I never knew your name."

She thought for a moment, then carefully felt in the pocket of the coat for the little bird and the piece of wood. She turned the little bird over in her hand. It was fine—rough and good at the same time. She stroked the feathers one last time. She wondered again who had made such a fine thing. She placed it in the palm of Barlach's open hand and closed his fingers around it. His hand was cold already. She had nothing else to give him.

She stood up to go, and was about to toss the other piece of wood into a corner when she changed her mind. It was just an old worthless piece of wood, but maybe she would keep it, and maybe someday she would carve something of her own. Maybe a bird.

She stayed with him until she sensed that his soul, hovering nearby, had flown away.

3:50 p.m.

When Alma emerged from the bell tower, she heard shouting and laughing, a sound she had never heard in the cathedral before. It filled the cathedral like music. The lost children of the crypt—the zombie-kids—streamed out of the doorway under the wooden podium.

"One, two, three, four . . ." Madame Jouet raised her voice as they swarmed around her. Her six—including Gabi, *mon Dieu*—and another five. She counted over and over.

"Happy name day, Gabi!" yelled Hannah and Roc.

Alma wanted to say goodbye before they all ran back to their homes. She'd be fine in her secret hiding place now that the tour guide was gone—but maybe they could come visit her once in a while. She watched them jostle and shove and bump each other like puppies, and then she turned away, not wanting to interrupt, and headed back down the aisle.

The sun had come out and colored light splashed through the cathedral, streaking the floor and pews and columns. Thunder rumbled softly in the distance, farther and farther away. It was a good place, and she wouldn't be so lonely after everyone left.

But she hadn't gone very far before the little crowd rolled into her from behind. They gathered her up, hugging and poking her as they did each other. Payah grabbed her hand and pulled her along toward the great doors. So much hugging.

Outside the cathedral, Madame hugged them all over again, counting and recounting. The five children who had homes rushed off to their families. Only Madame's children remained, leaping and jumping around the wet cathedral steps.

A *gendarme* arrived and he and Madame held a hushed conversation. Madame pointed to the bell tower and gestured. The *gendarme* hurried off.

Madame lowered herself to the wet stone with a sigh and patted her hair, wildly out of place. "My hat! Ah, but what is the loss of a hat when you find your children?"

Hannah stood before her and beckoned to Alma.

"Madame, this girl, Alma, she—"

Madame's head jerked up and a great range of feelings passed over her face in an instant. "But of course!" She heaved herself up. She wrapped her arms so tightly around Alma, the girl could hardly hear the steady stream of welcome.

Mercifully Hannah grabbed her hand and pulled her free. They ran down the cathedral steps and landed on the sidewalk with a splash.

Payah was trying out new names for herself with Roc. "Jasmine? Paquette? Sofia?"

He teased her. "Nougat? Melisande?"

Payah looked to Alma for help. Alma nodded encouragement and Payah smiled. "Payah, then," she said, and laughed her big, unexpected laugh. "A name all my own. For just me. Payah for short *and* for long." She jumped with both feet into a puddle.

Roc laughed. "Oh, all right, it's your name. *Vas-y,* Payah." He hoisted her onto his back for a ride. Alma thumped him good-naturedly on the head. Hannah linked her arm through Alma's. Together they led Madame Jouet home.